MERCILESS

BRYAN SMITH

GRINDHOUSE
PRESS

Grindhouse Press
PO BOX 521
Dayton, Ohio 45401

Grindhouse Press #055
ISBN-10: 1-941918-54-9
ISBN-13: 978-1-941918-54-8

Other titles by Bryan Smith

1

THE COUNTRYSIDE IN EAST TENNESSEE was beautiful in October. With Halloween right around the corner, yellow and burnt-orange leaves made the trees shrouding the winding roads of mountain country look festive and spooky. This was especially so in the early stages of twilight as shadows descended, the temperature dropped, and the wind whistled through the trees, stirring and scattering the falling leaves.

For newlyweds Grant Weatherby and Lindsey Harper, the scenic mountain vistas made for the perfect romantic backdrop as the second day of their long-planned journey across the continent drew to a close. They'd be spending tonight and the next two days at a cabin that had been in Grant's family for generations. Several sets of keys existed for the cabin and were passed around among various branches of the large, extended family throughout the year. A loose collective of elder family members kept track of when the property was occupied or available for use. Grant had reserved their time at the cabin and picked up the keys just last week. The cabin was still some dozen miles or so distant when Lindsey announced an urgent need to pee.

Grant frowned behind the wheel of the big Ford truck as he steered it along the winding route. "For real? You don't think you could hold it just a bit longer?"

Lindsey responded with a tight-lipped shake of her head. "Absolutely not. Sorry, but the need came over me all of a sudden. I feel like I might pee my pants if you don't stop and let me out."

Grant's frown deepened as his gaze swept both sides of the road. At first there was no obvious place to pull over. The road was narrow and the slight shoulder left little room for parking. Any vehicle coming up from behind them would have to swing out into the opposite lane temporarily to get around their truck and its large attached camper. With the sky getting progressively darker, it was too easy to imagine an oblivious truck driver slamming into their parked vehicle. Another factor was the road's many swoops and dips, which meant there were numerous blind spots along the route, a potentially deadly hazard.

Just as he was about to voice these concerns to his new wife, he took the truck around a bend in the road and spied an area a short way up ahead where the trees on the right thinned out and yielded to a roadside clearing.

He smiled as he glanced at Lindsey. "I was about to go on about how troublesome stopping anywhere along here would be, then lo and behold . . ."

The expression on his wife's face was a strained blend of tension and amusement as Grant eased the truck off the road and into the clearing. She muttered something about serendipity and bolted out the door before he could come to a full stop, making him realize she hadn't exaggerated the urgency of her need in the slightest.

The door on her side was standing open as he moved the gearshift over to P and cut the engine. Cool evening air drifted in, making him shiver slightly. He was in jeans and a short-sleeved Boston

University t-shirt, an outfit that had been more comfortable at the start of the day.

Leaving the keys in the ignition, he got out and gave the driver's side door a heave. The groan of the hinges as the door clunked shut was a reminder of the vehicle's vintage. He'd inherited the 1997 Ford and camper from his uncle, a lifelong bachelor who left no children behind upon passing seven months earlier. The late Carl Weatherby, Jr. had instead left a number of things to his only nephew, most of which Grant didn't give one shit about.

The truck and camper were another story, though.

The idea to roam the country with Lindsey once they were married came to him shortly after Carl's funeral. Grant and his bride-to-be had good jobs and some money saved up. Both had also accumulated quite a bit of vacation time. They were perfectly positioned to embark on an adventure of the sort usually reserved for either the very young or elderly retirees. Instead of jetting off to Jamaica or some other tropical destination for their honeymoon, they'd see the country from sea to shining sea, creating memories to last a lifetime. In the decades to come, they'd be telling and retelling their children and grandchildren all about it.

Lindsey was squatting above the ground with her back against the side of the truck not facing the road. Should anyone come driving around the bend in either direction, the angle would effectively shield her from view. She had her denim shorts down around her ankles as she relieved herself. Her eyes were closed and her head was tilted back as Grant approached from the other side of the truck.

He eyed her sleek legs and exposed ass and felt an unanticipated stirring of lust. Stirrings of lust for his wife happened on a regular basis, of course, but rarely in so awkward a setting. She opened her eyes when she sensed his presence and turned her head to smirk at him. He suddenly wanted to chew on that succulent bottom lip of hers more than anything.

She was done peeing.

Instead of pulling up her shorts when she stood, however, she kicked them away as she leaned against the side of the truck and started fingering herself. She made a noise of arousal and let out a heavy breath. "You could fuck me right here," she told him, voice turning husky. "No one would see."

Grant's cock stiffened as he watched Lindsey pleasure herself. "What if a cop comes along and decides to see what we're up to?"

She opened her eyes again and looked at him, her flushed features radiating pure lust. "Then we get a ticket for indecent exposure or whatever and have a crazy story to tell our friends. Or we have a threesome with the cop. Either way, I want you to fuck me right now."

Another sound of arousal escaped her lips, this one somehow more wanton and redolent of pure erotic need.

Grant went to her and did his best to give her what she wanted.

2

AFTER IT WAS OVER, THEY were in no hurry to travel the modest remaining distance to the cabin. The little roadside clearing struck both of them as a good place for some postcoital relaxation time, overlooking a little valley between hills as it did. They took a couple of lawn chairs from the camper and positioned them facing the hill on the other side of the valley. The last faint traces of daylight were visible just above the trees atop the other hill, a sliver of sky tinged a dark pink beneath the encroaching darkness.

Lindsey lit a joint and passed it to Grant after taking a single deep inhalation. He frowned as he put it to his lips and took a more modest hit. "Not sure what I think about this new penchant for risky behavior. First it's the public sex. Now we're smoking weed right out in the open."

Lindsey groaned as she leaned back in her chair and stretched her legs out in front of her. "Oh, relax," she said, smirking again as she glanced at him. "Not a single car has come by since we stopped here. It's like we have this whole corner of the world to ourselves."

"That could change at any time."

She laughed. "That's part of the thrill of it."

Grant took another small hit from the joint and passed it back to her. "If you say so."

"I do say so. And what I say goes."

She said it in a humorous way, but there was truth in her statement. His wife was a strong-willed woman accustomed to getting her way more often than not. Denying her what she wanted in any situation was a rare thing. Not that he had a problem with it. Even her wilder impulses led to fun experiences more often than not.

He waved the joint away when she tried passing it back to him. "No, thanks. I've still got some driving to do."

"Oh, come on, we're practically there already. And pot's basically legal now, so what's the big deal?"

Grant sighed. "Weed isn't legal everywhere yet. It definitely isn't in this state, by the way. Besides, this road is tricky even in daylight. I'd rather keep my wits about me until we get to the cabin."

"Fucking pussy."

Grant smiled in an indulgent way. "I like fucking *your* pussy."

Lindsey laughed.

Some silent moments elapsed as they watched that tinge of pink above the treetops continue to darken and fade away. Grant couldn't help marveling at how quiet it was out here in the country this time of year. In the summer, they'd be hearing a nearly constant buzzing of cicadas or the chirping of crickets, but the only sound of any significance at the moment remained the fall breeze stirring dead leaves.

Lindsey took yet another hit off the joint. "We should make it our mission to fuck in every state in the country. How many people can claim to have done that?"

Grant chuckled. "It'd give new meaning to the term 'sex tourism' anyway."

She nodded. "Hell yeah, it would. We'll save Hawaii for the end, a quick weekend flight out there and back before heading back to our mundane suburban existence."

Grant frowned. "I wouldn't call our lives mundane."

She yawned as she snuffed out the half-smoked joint by rubbing the lit end on an arm of the chair. "They are, though. This whole adventure aside, we're a prosperous but average white couple engaged in an ordinary existence. We're just like any other John and Mary Smith living on Everyday Avenue, with white picket fences as far as the eye can see." She smiled in the slightly wicked way she only ever showed him. "Except in that one special way. You know the one I mean."

Grant smiled, too. He did know.

His stomach growled.

Lindsey cocked an eyebrow as she glanced at him. "You sound as hungry as I feel. A good, hard fuck always get my appetite revving."

Grant nodded. "We should pack up and head on out to the cabin. Maybe grill some burgers or brats when we get there."

Lindsey rubbed her stomach and frowned. "Sounds good, but I'm hungry *now*. Let me at least get some crackers out of the camper before we move on."

Before Grant could say anything to that, they began to perceive the rumbling and clanking sound of a failing engine. It gave up the ghost with a final loud rattle as the vehicle came to a halt at the side of the road. Right at the edge of the clearing, from the sound of it.

After exchanging frowning glances, Grant and Lindsey got up to go take a look.

3

THE RUSTBUCKET PARKED JUST OFF the road looked even older than their truck. Twice as old, maybe. It was a decrepit-looking compact of indeterminate make, twin-tone in faded blue and red, a dirty piece of plastic sheeting covering the busted-out passenger side window. A man in a flannel shirt and dirty jeans got out of the car and popped the hood, lifting it up and propping it open with the built-in rod. He was in early middle-age and his brown skin indicated Hispanic heritage.

He peered at the engine in a way that struck Grant as obviously clueless. He made no attempt to reach in and touch anything or even lean in for a closer examination of the engine's ancient components. The man scratched the back of his neck and heaved a sigh audible from twenty feet or so away.

Lindsey nudged Grant with an elbow and leaned closer to whisper in his ear. "Check out this idiot and his hundred-dollar car. If he's a legal citizen, I'll eat a fucking hand grenade."

Grant lifted an eyebrow. "Wow. A hand grenade. That's a serious bet."

"Think I'm wrong?"

Grant shrugged. "Don't have an opinion one way or the other."

Lindsey smirked. "Okay, Mr. Noncommittal, how about this? Go over there and talk to him. Hear what he sounds like. If I'm right, you buy me something sparkly and expensive."

"And if you're wrong?"

"I'll do that really perverted thing you like," she said, still whispering. She put her mouth against his ear, tickling the lobe with her tongue. "You know, the one I've been withholding just to drive you crazy. You usually have to beg for it for weeks."

The elaboration was unnecessary. He'd known what she was talking about right away. His agreement was immediate: "It's a bet."

They could hear the man muttering in frustration as he continued to stare helplessly at the apparently dead engine. After another few moments of watching him, Lindsey leaned close and whispered in Grant's ear again. "Go talk to him. Keep him occupied. Where are the keys?"

Grant frowned. "They're in the truck. In the ignition. Why?"

She gave him a look of deep impatience as she started moving away from him. "Need to get in the camper for a minute. Just go talk to him, okay? Don't let him go anywhere."

Grant frowned harder. "But . . . why?"

"Just fucking do it."

"Fine."

Grant started off toward the man and his stalled car. Before he could get there, he heard the familiar groan of hinges as Lindsey opened one of the truck's doors to lean in and snatch the keys from the ignition. He didn't know what manner of chicanery his new bride had in mind, except that it likely involved messing with this stranger in some way. It was yet another example of her penchant for risky behavior. Thinking about it made him slightly nervous. He just hoped she wouldn't do anything too outrageous this time. At some point her luck would run out and she'd mess with the wrong person. An unstable or perhaps even mentally ill person.

He hoped today wasn't that day.

The man in the flannel shirt turned toward Grant as he drew to within a few feet of the shitty-looking car. His grin had a sheepish but amiable quality to it as they made eye contact. "Hey, man. I really hope you're more of a gearhead than I am. I've got no clue what I'm doing here."

Grant's expression was somewhere between a smile and an apologetic grimace. "I don't even know how to change my own oil. Sorry."

Inwardly, he was celebrating.

The so-called "perverted" thing he liked was definitely happening tonight. This guy sounded as all-American as a sitcom dad from the 1950s. He couldn't wait to see the look on Lindsey's face when she heard his voice.

The man nodded and rubbed at his patchy beard. "Figures. This useless bucket of bolts is probably beyond the help of even a skilled mechanic at this point, anyway. Imagine I'll have it hauled off to a junkyard. Guess I'll be on foot until I can get back to Danville."

Danville was the little town they'd passed through about ten miles back. This guy had clearly been headed somewhere in the other direction, but the next town down the road was another dozen miles at least beyond the turnoff that would take them up to their cabin. That would make it a journey of twenty-five miles or thereabouts from this spot.

"Hell of a walk ahead of you either way you go."

The man's features twisted in a pained-looking way, perhaps a reflection of the dread he felt at the prospect of walking that great a distance. "Yeah. Shit. Guess I better get started."

An awkward silence lasting several moments ensued. Grant's instinct was to offer the stranded motorist a ride back to Danville, but he knew Lindsey would not want to share traveling space with a complete stranger, especially this one. Not even for a relatively short ride. The offer therefore went unspoken.

Then he thought of something else, a way to help with minimal personal involvement. "Oh, shit. My phone. Surely they have a wrecker service back there in Danville. I could call you a tow truck."

The man's amiable grin returned. "That'd be a big help. I'd really appreciate it. Hey, maybe while we're at it, I could call my boss at the supermarket, too, let her know why I'll be so late getting there."

Grant nodded. "No problem. Happy to be of some kind of assistance, at least."

He dug into a hip pocket to drag out his phone.

"Hey, honey! That won't be necessary."

Both men turned toward the sound of Lindsey's voice.

She came striding rapidly toward them with a big smile on her face and a hand inside a white plastic bag. Grant recognized the bag as something she'd dug out of the trash in the camper. It'd originally contained snacks purchased recently at a convenience store. Now something heavier weighed it down.

Grant matched her expression with a strained grin of his own. He was a little on edge due to still having no idea what she was up to. "Hey, babe. We were just about to call a wrecker."

She was within six feet of them when she said, "Like I already said, that won't be necessary."

Grant glanced at the Hispanic guy and saw right away he was already transfixed by Lindsey's piercing blue eyes. Her ability to disarm nearly anyone of the male persuasion with one smiling look was like a superpower. It was the main reason so many never saw the hidden streak of cruelty beneath the pretty facade.

"Unlike my husband, I know a thing or two about cars. Pretty sure I can get your motor running."

Grant barely managed not to snort at that last comment. The not-so-subtle innuendo behind her words was no accident, and was yet another practically infallible method of distraction. In those moments, the guy wasn't thinking about his broken-down car or being late for work. He was thinking only of Lindsey and her luscious body.

The man cleared his throat and blushed a little as he said, "Oh, hey, that would be awesome."

Lindsey glanced at her husband. "Step back, babe. You're out of your depth here. Sorry, but you know it's true."

Grant shrugged and moved several feet away without a word.

The stranger frowned as his gaze focused on the plastic bag. "What do you have there?"

Lindsey laughed. "Something fun. Check it out."

Grant felt a sharp pang of apprehension as her hand came out of the bag.

Oh, shit.

The stranger's frown deepened as he stared at the thing in her hand. "What is that? That's not real, is it?"

Lindsey said nothing.

She aimed the tranquilizer gun at the man's chest and squeezed the trigger.

4

THE OTHER ITEMS IN THE white bag were two rolls of duct tape. The two rolls constituted a small percentage of their unusually large supply of the stuff, the rest of which was still stowed away in the camper. Once Lindsey had removed them, she allowed the empty bag to float away in the breeze. She tossed one roll to Grant before dropping to her knees to flip the unconscious man over onto his stomach. He was heavy, so Grant had to help her. Using the tape, she went to work securing the man's hands together behind his back.

At his wife's direction, Grant simultaneously did the same with the man's ankles. Though he was shocked by what she'd done, there was no taking it back, and arguing about it with her while they were still in clear view of anyone who might come driving by was clearly a waste of time. Getting this guy tied up and stowed away out of sight in the camper was priority number one for now. Any debate regarding her actions could wait until after that. So he went about his work without comment, focusing only on doing the job properly to ensure the stranger wouldn't be able to kick free of his bonds. He was certain Lindsey was doing the same as she secured his wrists.

As soon as they were finished, they grabbed hold of the stranger at either end and heaved him up off the ground. Grunting from the exertion, they carried him over to the camper as quickly as they could manage. The back door was standing open and Lindsey had put the steps down. Grant was grateful for that, at least. Wasting more precious time setting the man down and picking him up again while they got the camper open would've sucked.

Grant sighed in relief as they made it into the camper before another vehicle could come along. He was breathing heavily when they dropped the still-unconscious stranger on the floor. "Why . . . the hell . . . did you do that?"

She frowned. "What do you mean?"

"I mean . . . I thought we discussed this. We agreed we wouldn't try it until we got to the end of our trip."

She gave him an impatient look as she opened one of the camper's many storage cabinets, from which she plucked out a pair of lace black panties. He knew it was the same pair she'd been wearing all day. Evidently she'd taken the time to remove them while inside the camper a few minutes ago. "We'll talk about that as soon as we're back on the road. Let me finish here."

The unconscious stranger was on his back now. Kneeling next to him, Lindsey forced his mouth open and pushed the panties in between his lips. She then tore off a strip of duct tape and smoothed it into place over his mouth.

"Why the panties?"

She shrugged as she stood up. "I just liked the idea of it. Gives the whole thing kind of a kinky edge. You definitely like it when I do it to you."

"The difference is you're not gonna fuck this guy."

Lindsey didn't respond to that as she stepped over the stranger's unmoving form and moved toward the back of the camper. "Come on. We need to get moving."

Grant sighed in exasperation. Her impulsiveness bothered him, as it left them susceptible to all kinds of potential unforeseen complications. A thing like this required careful planning and execution. As speedily as they'd worked together, this was just sloppy.

He followed her out of the camper and around to the side of the truck facing away from the road, where she'd already folded up the lawn chairs. She had one in each hand. He offered to take one for her as she again headed to the back of the camper, but she shook this off and told him to pick up his empty beer bottle. He was about to ask why when the obvious reason occurred to him. The bottle had his fingerprints on it. As he knelt to scoop up the bottle, he heard the rattle of the chairs being tossed into the camper. Next he heard Lindsey putting the retractable steps back and closing the door.

He carried the empty bottle with him as he got back behind the wheel of the truck. Lindsey took it from him and tossed him the keys as she climbed in on the other side and closed the door. "Get our asses out of here."

Grant put the key in the ignition and started the engine, shifting gears even as he glanced at her. "You still owe me an explanation."

A worry line creased her forehead as she leaned forward and glanced out at the road. "And you'll get one, honey, but I want to be away from this place first. So fucking hurry, okay?"

Grant reluctantly acknowledged the wisdom of what she was saying. He was impatient to know why she'd done this now instead of waiting to do it in a more organized way in a more controlled environment. But she was right. At some point, the guy they'd taken would be reported missing. News reports might include a description of the man's broken-down car. Allowing a witness to later recall seeing that car and their camper together in the same clearing would obviously be a very bad thing.

He hit the accelerator and the old Ford surged to the edge of the road where he paused a moment to glance back and check for approaching cars. Still nothing in either direction, which seemed almost miraculous at this point. He eased the truck out onto the road and hit the gas again, speeding away from the clearing. Checking his mirrors several seconds later, he saw it had disappeared entirely from view.

Letting out a relieved breath, he relaxed his grip on the steering wheel and settled back in his seat.

He glanced again at his beautiful bride, who was visibly more relaxed now. She was smiling in a contented way as she stared at the passenger side mirror.

"Okay, Lindsey. Spill your guts."

5

TAKING ANOTHER HUMAN BEING'S LIFE had always been a key component of their long-planned trip across the country. It was an idea borne out of their shared fascination with serial killers and true crime in general, which was one of the big things they'd bonded over during the early stages of their romance. In the beginning, this had seemed benign enough. After all, it was a fascination shared by countless others, the vast majority of whom would never dream of committing such crimes themselves.

Until falling in love with Lindsey, Grant had always considered himself in that category of people who would only ever read about murders instead of actually committing them. True crime documentaries and books were more than sufficient to feed his morbid fascination. He had a good life and had no interest in blowing it up by doing something stupid and potentially winding up on death row.

That changed three months into his relationship with Lindsey when, after a particularly frenzied bout of lovemaking, they discussed the latest multi-part murder documentary they'd just finished bingeing on Netflix. In the midst of this conversation, Lindsey confessed to harboring for years a fantasy to kidnap and kill someone. Grant didn't take this seriously at first. It was a fantasy. People had all kinds of crazy fantasies. As long as they didn't do the truly crazy things in real life, where was the harm in that? So he played along, telling her he harbored similar fantasies.

In the ensuing months, they kept talking about it and the fantasies Lindsey described became more elaborate. It became clear to Grant she had given a great deal of serious thought to the real practicalities of how to kill a person and get away with it. Even then, he didn't believe she had any genuine intent of doing it. They took up roleplaying in the bedroom, mostly kidnap scenarios featuring him as the victim. He spent a lot of time tied to their bed while she beat him and threatened to torture and kill him if he failed to satisfy her sexually. The kinky and sometimes violent roleplay didn't bother him because he thought of it as a safe outlet for channeling and purging their darker desires.

Six months into their relationship, the day after his proposal of marriage, she gave him what amounted to an ultimatum. She would only accept the proposal if he agreed to help make her murder fantasy a reality. Her body language and stern tone of voice finally convinced him of her seriousness. She really wanted to do this. Commit a murder. Kill an innocent human being for no reason other than pleasure. Upon realizing this, Grant felt a reflexive sense of horror, but this faded quickly. He realized he wasn't as bothered by the idea as most people would be. And above all else, he did not want to lose the woman he considered the love of his life.

So here they were.

Agreeing to help her actualize her fantasy was his wedding gift to her. Lindsey called it their "gift to each other", but whatever.

Several more quiet moments went by as they continued at a rapid rate down the winding road.

Unable to take her silence any longer, Grant rolled his eyes in exasperation and shouted, "Lindsey!"

His louder tone finally snapped her out of her reverie. She was still smiling as she sat up straighter and looked at him. "What, baby?"

He sighed. "You said you would explain."

She nodded. "Yeah. Sorry. Got caught up in thinking about things."

By Grant's estimation, they were now about ten miles away from the private access road that would lead up to the old family cabin. Things seemed more or less under control now, but he'd feel a lot better about the whole situation once they were on private land. The odds of a nosy cop stopping them and asking to take a peek inside the camper were already low. He was riding the speed limit and there was no probable cause for a search anyway. The truck was old, but everything about it was in proper working condition, with no malfunctioning tail lights or anything else of the sort warranting a pullover. There was no reason to think they'd be anything other than fine as long as he kept his wits about him this last little stretch of the way.

His eyes went back to the road as he said, "Care to share what you're thinking? Because I'm really confused about pretty much everything right now."

Lindsey lifted her shoulders in a small shrug. "Okay, look, I know it's not the way we talked about doing it. I'm sorry I didn't discuss it with you beforehand, but it was an impulse and there was no time for that."

Grant shook his head and sighed heavily again, not bothering to hide his dismay. "Come on, Lindsey, we talked about this. We'd only do this in a carefully planned way because—"

She nodded, scowling. "Yes, yes, yes, I fucking know, okay? Acting on impulse with something like this is bad and dangerous. You're absolutely right about that. We did agree on it, and I'm sorry I broke the rules. But, baby, I just couldn't help it." She paused briefly to heave a breath and collect her thoughts. "Okay, listen . . . and I know this will sound flaky as hell, but whatever. When that guy showed up in his pathetic junker, with nobody else around, I took it as a sign. A moment of serendipity. Like he was meant to come along at that exact time and we were meant to take him. It was like he was a gift from the universe or something."

Grant nodded slowly.

He said nothing for several silent moments. Her argument boiled down to excuse-making disguised as something deep and meaningful. She wanted what she wanted when she wanted it. Simple as that. All he could do now was move forward and hope to keep her from doing anything as risky as that again.

6

BACK THERE AT THE ROADSIDE clearing, a couple of elements came together in Lindsey's mind at almost precisely the same moment. First and foremost, the commitment they'd already made to taking a human life together. Nothing would have happened without that agreement already solidly entrenched in her psyche. Their proximity to a private place where they would be free to do whatever they wanted with their captive was, however, the deciding factor.

This is what she told Grant.

She described it as a perfect storm situation, a set of circumstances so ideal for indulging in her darkest fantasies she couldn't help but take action. The nearest neighbors were miles distant. There would be no one around to hear the man's screams or pleas for mercy.

She laughed. "Seriously, what's the big deal? We're already planning to murder at least one person. For no reason other than the sheer enjoyment of it. Once you've gotten to that place in your head, why put it off needlessly? There's literally no good reason we had to wait until the end of the trip. And the sooner we go ahead and do it, the freer we'll be. I'm talking about *real* freedom, Grant, freedom in its purest fucking form. We should seize the moment and revel in that. Hell, we're already doing it. This is exciting, baby. A dream come fucking true. Please try to enjoy it with me."

What she was saying made some level of sense, at least from a certain deranged perspective. Despite arriving at this conclusion, Grant nonetheless experienced a high level of apprehension as they arrived at the gated private access drive and came to a stop. His mind was buzzing as he got out of the truck and approached the gate, which was the bar type mounted to a pole. He dropped his keys several feet shy of arriving at the gate and had to stop and kneel to pick them up.

When he glanced back at the truck, Lindsey was staring at him in a way that was neither impatient nor serene. On the surface, it was an emotionless blank. She was observing him in the dispassionate manner of a scientist studying a microbe on a slide. It gave him a small case of the creeps. Probably this was just him allowing stress and paranoia to get the better of him.

He gave her a little wave and continued to the gate.

His burgeoning paranoia was a result of certain subtle implications he'd picked up on in her little speech . . .

. . . *at least one person* . . .

It was hard not to interpret that as leaving the door open for more murders in the future. Yes, a promise had been made. Their honeymoon murder would be the only one they'd ever commit, a final way of bonding at the deepest, most intimate level. Something they could always look back on with secret fondness as they grew old together, that shared knowledge of how far they were willing to go for each other. In a way, it would be a more solemn and sacred thing than the vows they'd exchanged at their wedding.

At this point, however, it didn't feel far-fetched to believe she might come away from this experience with a genuine taste for murder. She might, in fact, decide she enjoyed it so much she wanted to do it again and again.

The bar gate was secured by a padlock and a heavy length of rust-flecked chain. Grant found the duplicate key he'd been given by an elderly relative a day before setting out on their trip. He slid it into the padlock and unlocked it. After pulling the old length of chain clear of the slat holding it in place, he pulled the bar open wide enough to allow access. He then got back in the truck and drove it through the opening onto the private drive. With that accomplished, he got out again briefly to close and lock the gate.

The drive was a rutted dirt road that rose sharply on a narrow and winding mountain ridge. There were steep drop-offs to either side, which became more potentially hazardous the higher up they went. The truck's old suspension bounced and loudly creaked in a way that steadily became more unsettling. There were no guardrails along the sides of the road, a fact of which Grant was intensely aware as he steered them up the road toward the cabin, which he still couldn't see. Right then, all he cared about was avoiding a calamitous plunge down into the tree-covered valley below.

When they finally arrived on level ground and the cabin came into view, Grant let out a relieved breath along with a whispered thank you to whatever deity or power was responsible for seeing them safely to their destination. Here was where the mountain ridge ended, on a much wider piece of land. The cabin was at the back of a large clearing ringed by tall trees. Fading sunlight glinted off rooftop solar panels. Out back was a large generator for backup power and a massive water tank. All the cozy comforts of home in the middle of nowhere. Grant loved this place. After he parked the truck parallel to the long porch, he shut the engine off and they got out of the truck.

With full darkness encroaching, there was close to zero chance of anyone observing them as they transferred the man they'd abducted from the camper to the cabin. Even in broad daylight, the cabin's isolation would've made this virtually impossible.

Grant took a few steps out into the clearing and allowed himself a few moments to take in the gorgeous mountain scenery, which was still faintly visible thanks to the last lingering traces of daylight. In just another few minutes, the last of that light would be gone and the landscape would disappear under a cloak of darkness. He imagined sitting out on the cabin's porch in the middle of the night surrounded by all that inky, impenetrable blackness and felt a chill.

There couldn't be a more perfect place to do the awful things they had in mind.

7

BY THE TIME THEY WERE able to get the stranger out of the camper and into the cabin, he was showing signs of regaining consciousness. He groaned and weakly mumbled something unintelligible after they dumped him on the floor of the main room.

Lindsey squatted next to him and snapped her fingers over his face, making him blink slowly and squint at her through red-rimmed eyes. "Hey there, sleepyhead. We're about to get the fun started. Aren't you excited?"

He groaned again and forced his eyes open wider after his eyelids started drooping again. The gag muffled the words he tried to say, but it sounded like, "Where am I?"

Lindsey laughed. "Where are you? You're at the end of the fucking line. This is it for you, pendejo."

Still squatting above him, she craned her head around, surveying the interior of the cabin. She'd never been here before and had been expecting something like the type of dilapidated cabin she'd seen in so many horror movies, a rickety old hovel barely fit for human habitation, but this place was nice. There'd never been any rational foundation for the internalized image. The Weatherbys were well-off people in general. They wouldn't spend their mountain getaways in some falling-down old tin shack. She nonetheless felt vaguely let down.

The main room was wide open and spacious, with a large, L-shaped leather sofa and leather recliner facing an enormous wall-mounted flatscreen TV to the left as one came in through the front door. Elsewhere was a large area clearly meant for dining and recreation and a recessed kitchen nook that was also far bigger than she'd expected. A set of sturdy-looking bookshelves was stuffed-to-bursting with old board games. Beyond where the sofa and TV were situated was a wooden staircase leading to the second floor where she assumed the bedrooms were. A glance up at the second-floor landing appeared to confirm this, with multiple closed doors visible on the other side of the unpainted wooden railing. Of particular interest was how clean the place was. There was very little in the way of dust anywhere.

The man on the floor groaned again and struggled to lift his bound hands toward her in a pitifully beseeching way. Lindsey snapped a finger against his nose, making him flinch. "Hey, honey, how often does this place get used? It's so goddamn clean."

Grant came closer and peered down at the bound man, his expression mildly curious. He shrugged. "I think Justin and Kurt were here last week."

Justin was Grant's bisexual first cousin, and Kurt was the guy he was currently dating. Lindsey had fucked both of them in a wild, drunken threesome two days before her wedding to Grant. There were pictures of Justin taking her from behind stored away in a secret online photo album.

She made a face and shook her head in a display of disgust. "Ugh. I hate those guys. But the cleanliness makes sense now. You know how queers are."

Grant flinched at the comment. "Uh . . . isn't that a bit of a big-oted stereotype?"

Lindsey smirked as she stood up. "We're about to torture and kill a man and you're worried about my lack of cultural sensitivity?"

He shrugged, looking a little sheepish now. "I don't really care, I guess. It's just a bit of a surprise. You're always so into how woke you are on social media."

She laughed. "Baby, that shit is all for show. It's a mask, a way to make people think I'm normal and caring. The truth is, I don't give a shit about anybody in this world other than you and me. I hate all people of all races, genders, and sexual orientations."

"Huh."

She rolled her eyes and made her lips pouty as she approached her husband and pulled him into a light embrace. "Don't be that way. I can see the wheels spinning in your head. You think I've been dishonest with you."

He shrugged but didn't attempt to pull out of the embrace. "More like you chose not to show me everything behind the mask. You didn't have to do that. I could've handled it." He glanced in a pointed way at the bound man on the floor. "I mean, I'm going along with this, right?"

She smiled broadly a moment before pressing herself against him and kissing him lustily on the mouth for several seconds before pulling away again. "You're right, baby. I shouldn't have kept that part of me hidden from you. No more secrets. That's a promise. Now do me a favor and go fetch the rest of the duct tape from the camper. The toolbox, too. I want to get started on this guy."

He nodded, smiling. "Be right back."

Lindsey's smile vanished the moment he was out the door. She turned away from the door, which Grant had left open, and again squatted above their captive. He was close to fully awake now, star-ing up at her, eyes brimming with tears. Her face remained an emo-tionless blank as she grabbed the crotch of his jeans and squeezed.

He gasped in terror, apparently certain she was about to begin the torture by crushing his balls, but that was not her intent here. She massaged his genitals through the fabric of his jeans the way she would with any man she was attempting to turn on. At first there was no physical response and the look on his face conveyed a deep level of confusion, but she kept at it and in another moment she began to feel a slight stiffening of his cock. She was sure he would've soon become fully erect, but she took her hand away and stood up when she heard Grant mounting the creaky steps to the porch.

Turning away from the captive, her smile returned as soon as Grant came through the door and kicked it shut behind him. "That took a while. Everything okay out there?"

Grant was frowning again as he carried the toolbox and a medium-sized cardboard box filled with rolls of duct tape over to the dining area and set them on the table there. "Took me a few minutes to find the toolbox. It wasn't where I thought I put it. Had to hunt around a bit." He sighed and shook his head. "Unusual memory lapses bug me. Can't help thinking of my grandmother when shit like that happens."

This was a reference to Grammy Evelyn, his grandmother on his mother's side of the family. The woman had suffered from Alzheimer's for years before passing away last year.

The corners of her mouth drew down in an expression of sympathy as she said, "Oh, Grant, honey, you've got years and years to go before you have to seriously worry about anything like that."

Grant was a young man, so this was almost certainly true. Besides, she knew he hadn't suffered any kind of memory lapse. She'd intentionally switched the toolbox to a different storage cabinet during her time alone in the camper back at the roadside clearing. This was a carefully calculated move to allow her an early private moment with the captive. It'd worked out precisely as she'd foreseen.

"Come on, help me get him into one of those chairs."

Arranged around the table was a set of four identical chairs, the seats of each chair pushed up under the table. Grant pulled one of them out and turned it so it was facing away from the table. Each of them then grabbed their captive under an arm and heaved him up. The toes of his work boots skidded across the wooden floor as they dragged him over to the dining area and slowly lowered him down onto the sturdily built chair, taking care to slide his already bound hands over the back of the chair. Although the man was conscious now, he remained somewhat woozy from the sedation drug still circulating in his system. His eyes looked glassy and his head kept lolling to the side.

Lindsey used duct tape to lash the man's ankles to the legs of the chair. After that, she wound thick layers of tape around the length of his legs up to his knees, a job that required the use of two full rolls of duct tape. With another roll, she fully encased his hands in tape, then used another to bind his arms to the slats of the chair's back. After taking a moment to check out her work, she judged it satisfactory.

They were about ready to carry out their first kill together. An important distinction. *Together.* This would be Grant's first kill, but it would be her second. The first had happened several years ago.

That she'd already previously killed a person was another of the many things Grant still didn't know about her. Back in college, she'd been getting high on the roof of a nightclub with a girl she'd met in the bathroom only minutes earlier. Rooftop access was technically barred to patrons, but the girl knew how to get up there anyway. They were all alone up there as they made out and did multiple bumps of coke. Lindsey didn't actually like coke, but it felt like the thing to do in the moment. At one point the girl went over to the edge of the roof and said something vapid about how beautiful the city looked at night. On impulse, Lindsey shoved her off the roof and the girl fell to her death on the sidewalk below.

Lindsey hurried back the way she'd come and slipped out of the nightclub without making eye contact with anyone. She was pretty sure no one had seen her in the company of the girl she'd just killed. They hadn't spent any time together at the bar or out on the dance floor. There'd been no one else in the bathroom with them when they met. The girl was powerfully attracted to her and impulsively proffered an invitation that wound up leading to her death. There was nothing at all to connect them. Those first weeks after the incident were nonetheless tense as she dreaded a knock on the door from the cops, but that never happened and soon she realized she was in the clear.

Technically, she was lying to Grant by allowing him to believe this would be her first foray into the world of murder, but in spirit she was being more or less sort of truthful. That first time had been sheer impulse, nothing more. There'd been no time to wallow in it or savor the terror felt by her victim. This was different. This would be her first premeditated murder, something she'd dreamed of most of her life. She would have all the time she wanted to revel in this man's fear and agony. The anticipation of it was almost painfully sweet.

Lindsey got to her feet and moved around to take a look at their captive from the front. The fear in his watery eyes was a joy to behold.

Grant was standing next to her now.

She gave him a sidelong smile and said, "Well, what should we do to him first?"

8

RIGHT UP TO THE MOMENT she asked that question, Grant had for the most part thought of the planned murder in abstract terms, like a shared exercise in fantasy or make-believe. Not that much different from their bedroom roleplaying, really. Thinking of it the way he had was a psychological defense mechanism, a means of keeping the hard reality of it at arm's length until that was no longer possible.

Well, that moment of reckoning had arrived. There could no longer be any turning away from what was about to happen. He stared at the man strapped to the chair and tried to imagine himself using the things in the toolbox on him. The guy was utterly helpless and thus would be unable to evade or defend himself against, for instance, a hammer blow to the face. As he thought about it, Grant could almost feel the weight of that hammer in his hand. He was thinking about how it would feel to swing the hammer and have it connect with vulnerable human flesh when he realized his hands were shaking. Not wanting Lindsey to see how nervous he was, he curled his hands into fists in an effort to still the shaking.

"I asked you a question."

Grant flinched at the sound of Lindsey's voice. "Sorry," he said, glancing at her with a strained smile tugging at the edges of his mouth. "I spaced out a little. Daydreaming about what we're about to do, I guess."

She frowned. "You're sweating."

"Am I?" He rubbed a hand across his brow, then frowned at his glistening palm. "Huh. Sorry, I guess I'm nervous."

"You're not having second thoughts, are you?"

She turned fully toward him as she said this, giving him a hard look that made her opinion of that possibility clear. It was all he needed to know there would be no backing out of this regardless of how he responded to her question. Even if he declared an intent not to participate in the torture side of the proceedings, the bottom line would not change. Things had gone too far for that. The man they'd taken would die in this cabin.

Grant shook his head. "No. Definitely not."

She nodded, that stern expression still firmly in place. "Good. You know how much this means to me. Backing out at this point would put our marriage in serious jeopardy. It'd be a betrayal. Do you get that?"

He nodded in the most emphatic way possible, eager to please. "Yes, yes, I do. Like I said, I'm sorry. But I'm human, you know? This is a big thing. Some jittery nerves are to be expected."

Lindsey's expression turned a shade harder, an indication her anger was still escalating despite his reassurances. She moved a step closer. "We spent months and months talking endlessly about this. I'd hate to think you were misleading me all along."

Grant's cheeks flushed red as he absorbed the brunt of her anger. He palmed more sweat away from his brow and wiped it on his jeans. "I wasn't misleading you, I swear. Please cut me some slack for my nerves. I'll get over it. I promise."

Still glaring at him, she said, "You better."

She went to the table, opened the toolbox, and began sorting through the things inside it. The man in the chair flinched at the sound of metal things clanking against each other. Whimpering sounds were audible from behind his gag. Grant made eye contact with him for a moment before tearing his gaze away. The pleading look in the man's eyes made his stomach clench. Maybe he didn't have what it took to go through with something like this, after all.

Didn't matter, though.

He was trapped with absolutely no way out.

Lindsey's hand came out of the toolbox as she turned away from the table and moved into place behind their captive. Gripped in her right hand was a pair of wire cutters, with the snips open. She placed a hand gently on the bound man's shoulder. He jerked at the moment of contact, the volume of his whimpering sharply increasing. He turned his head in a futile effort to see what she was up to.

"Face forward, you piece of shit." Lindsey's hand came away from his scalp and she gave him a hard swat upside the head, making him yelp in pain. "We're just getting started here. You should save your energy for when things get really bad. Understand?"

Still whimpering softly, he nodded and sniffled.

Lindsey smiled. "Good. Because make no fucking mistake about it, things are about to get very, very bad for you indeed."

She pulled his right earlobe away from the side of his head, applied the snips to the stretched-out bit of flesh, and clipped it off. Blood leaked from the wound and spilled down his neck to his chest as he screamed in agony behind the gag. Lindsey again swatted him upside the head and screamed at him to shut up unless he wanted to move on to the genital torture phase of the proceedings much sooner than planned. This threat did manage to cow him into suppressing the urge to scream. The screams, however, were replaced by a continuous loud whimpering, which Lindsey appeared to deem at least temporarily acceptable.

For a while, she stood there smirking down at him from behind, clearly enjoying her victim's misery every bit as much as she'd always claimed she would. For Lindsey, nothing remotely resembling a second thought had ever crossed her mind. Grant knew that beyond any doubt now. The look on her face was sheer malicious glee. Just as the man's whimpering began to subside ever so slightly, she pinched his wounded ear and gave it a hard twist, laughing as his screams resumed. She allowed the screaming to go on a few moments before again swatting him multiple times and reminding him what would happen next if he didn't stop.

The captive needed a bit longer this time to regain some semblance of control, but he finally managed it. His flushed face was sheened in sweat and his eyes danced wildly in their sockets, desperately seeking some sign of help or hope from somewhere. Of course, nothing of the sort was forthcoming.

Lindsey stepped out from behind the chair and showed the man the bloody bit of severed flesh, holding it inches away from his face. "See that? That used to be part of you. It's not anymore. Isn't that a fucking trip? Hey, watch this."

She backed off a few steps and dropped the earlobe on the floor, grinding it to mush beneath the heel of her shoe. Tears streamed down the man's face as he watched her do this. Lindsey laughed wildly at the sight of the man's tears. The sound struck Grant as not far removed from the exaggerated maniacal cackling of a crazy person in an old movie. The churning in his stomach was getting steadily worse.

Then Lindsey abruptly stopped laughing and turned around, slapping the wire cutters into Grant's hand.

Grinning broadly, she said, "Your turn, baby."

9

GRANT'S HAND WAS SHAKING AS he tightly gripped the padded handles of the wire cutters. Lindsey gripped his hand and held it until the shaking began to subside. His face was still red, and he was again sweating profusely.

"Grant, honey, just breathe, okay?" She said this with a more soothing and less reproachful tone than before. These symptoms of a lack of fortitude in her partner remained worrisome, but another display of anger at this critical juncture might only make things worse. The anger was still there beneath the surface, but she managed to hold it in by telling herself it was too soon to give up on him being able to see this thing through with her. It was clear he wasn't as strong mentally as she was, but that didn't mean he was a lost cause. He needed guidance, that was all. Guidance and the firm, steadying hand of the love of his life, as he often described her.

He swallowed with noticeable difficulty before hoarsely saying, "Okay."

She smiled, maintaining the tight grip on his hand. It was no longer shaking, but she sensed now was not the time to let go. The physical contact was his emotional anchor. She imagined waves of strengthening energy transferring from herself to her husband, charging him up like a battery.

"Good. That's good, baby. Now I want you to do something for me, okay?"

He nodded. "Okay."

His face was no longer quite so bright a shade of scarlet now. She could feel him continuing to calm down. He just needed a little extra babying to get him to a place in his head where he could do this. "I want you to close your eyes. Can you do that for me?"

Grant sighed heavily and did as instructed. "Okay," he said again, his tone somewhat less brittle than before. "I'm sorry about this."

She let go of his hand and was pleased to see the shaking did not resume. Now her hand went to his shoulder and gently gripped it as she said, "It's okay. There's nothing to be sorry about. I love you and we're in this together. There's nothing to fear because I'll be with you every step of the way. Together we are powerful. Unstoppable. There's nothing we can't do. There's nothing *you* can't do. Do you believe me?"

The redness was continuing to fade from his face and he was no longer sweating buckets. The way he was responding to her efforts to soothe and reassure him renewed her faith in him, at least partially. The true test of his mettle as a possible killing partner was still ahead. All would be well if she could get him to inflict a bit of genuine grievous bodily harm on the man they'd taken without having a breakdown.

If anything resembling a total breakdown occurred, she had a bleak contingency plan to which she did not wish to resort, mainly because it would mean involving the police and engaging in a lot of serious play-acting. She'd spent her entire life pretending to be a normal human being with normal emotions and had gotten pretty good at it. Feigning a crushing level of grief over the death of her husband at the hands of the murderous stranger who'd abducted them, however, would require the acting performance of a lifetime.

Convincingly selling that scenario to the cops would exhaust her mentally, but she believed it was something she could do. It would be an absolutely last-ditch thing, though. While she didn't "love" Grant in the traditional way—because she was incapable of truly feeling that emotion—she did feel deeply attached to him. He was the only person to whom she'd ever dared expose the darker areas of her mind. They had shared interests in some of those areas, and he hadn't reacted in horror when she'd confessed her desire to murder. That in itself was a miracle of sorts.

Grant nodded. "I believe you. And, Lindsey . . ."

Lindsey waited a beat after he trailed off before saying, "Yes, dear?"

With his eyes still closed, he said, "I love you more than anything. There's nothing I wouldn't do for you."

Hearing him say this pleased her and gave her additional hope, but the important stuff was still ahead. "I feel exactly the same, honey. Now keep your eyes closed and walk with me."

He was no longer perspiring at all as he swallowed again and let out a breath. "Okay."

She directed a smirk at the quivering and whimpering man tied to the chair as she walked with Grant, savoring the terror in his eyes like a fine wine. Her nipples stiffened as she felt a renewed surge of arousal. She dug her fingers into Grant's shoulder a little harder than intended as she steered him into position behind the captive. It seemed hard to believe, but less than an hour had passed since they'd fucked against the side of the truck in that clearing. He probably wasn't quite ready to go again just yet, but there were other things they could do that didn't involve his cock penetrating her vagina.

But first things first.

She relaxed her grip on his shoulder without taking her hand away. "Okay, Grant. Open your eyes."

His eyes fluttered open. "Okay. Now what?"

After lingering behind him a moment longer while libidinous thoughts continued to dance through her head, she found her focus again and took her hand from his shoulder. In another moment, she was standing in front of the chair, facing her husband and their helpless captive.

Lindsey smiled. "Later on, things will get too messy for this to matter, but what I'm interested in right now is symmetry. Shorten his other ear. Make it match the other one."

Grant allowed himself another moment to get as mentally centered as he could manage and then he did it. He stretched out the man's left earlobe and, with a snip of the wire cutters, it came away from the side of his head. A fresh rivulet of blood instantly began streaming down the side of his neck. His screams resumed in that same moment and he again began bucking uselessly against his bonds.

Lindsey laughed and clapped her hands together. "You did it! Congratulations, babe."

A small smile curved the corners of his mouth as he made eye contact with her. "I did, didn't I? Holy shit."

After laughing gleefully a bit longer, Lindsey sighed in relief. She was glad she would not have to kill the man she'd just married tonight. Unbeknownst to him, he'd passed the most important test of his life.

10

NOW THAT IT WAS DONE, a tremendous weight came off Grant's shoulders. He allowed himself an inward moment to assess how he was reacting at a physical level, fearing a return of the stomach trouble that had plagued him in the moments leading up to Lindsey's intervention. To his immense relief, he detected no symptoms of physical disturbance. No more shaking or sweating like a pig, either. In the moments that followed, he realized he was also experiencing nothing discernible in the way of psychological distress. No traces of the moral quandary he'd wrestled with such a short while ago remained.

Lindsey was laughing and soon he began to laugh, too. He felt so much better knowing for certain he could go through with this. Taking that first step had been harder than he'd ever imagined, but now that it was behind him, he felt reinvigorated and eager to embark on the rest of this blood-soaked adventure with his daring and exhilarating partner.

Flicking the bloody sliver of flesh away with an uncaring gesture, he turned away from the bound man and dumped the wire cutters in the open toolbox. He spent some time sorting through the other implements inside it while Lindsey went into the kitchen nook and opened a cabinet. She fetched an old dishrag from a lower shelf and then made her way over to the living area. Grant glanced that way in time to see her wiping the bloody earlobe off the back of the sofa, where it had adhered to the leather upholstery.

Still sorting through the items in the toolbox, he glanced her way and smiled. "Sorry, I wasn't thinking."

Lindsey shrugged. "We gotta be more careful, babe. Obviously we're gonna have a helluva cleanup job ahead of us before we leave here, but we should be careful not to lose track of anything too incriminating."

He chuckled, nodding. "Such as stray body parts."

"Exactly. And that goes for me, too." She directed a glance at the place on the floor where she'd ground the man's other earlobe to mush, then frowned when she again met his gaze. "We should really have a tarp or piece of plastic sheeting under that chair."

Grant cocked an eyebrow at her, giving her a gently reproachful look. "Well, you know, originally we weren't planning to do this until much later on. That included waiting to acquire certain supplies until we were on the other side of the country."

She gave him a sour, slightly sneering look. "Yeah, yeah, I know. I broke the fucking rules and did exactly what we agreed we wouldn't do. It's all my fault. I'm sorry, okay?"

He smiled warmly at her. In the aftermath of what he'd done, he felt closer to her than ever. She truly was the love of his life. "It's okay. You got excited, that's all. What's done is done. Maybe there's something we could use in the shed out back. If not, I'm sure there's some spare blankets upstairs. That'd be better than nothing. We could take them with us and burn them later."

Her face registered distaste. "Ew. I don't want to go poking around in some nasty old shed. I'll go check upstairs."

She came over and gave him a quick kiss on the mouth before trotting over to the set of wooden steps and beginning her ascent to the second floor. He watched the sexy movement of her incredible ass in those tight denim shorts as she climbed the steps and felt a fresh stirring of desire. It'd been maybe an hour since their bout of impromptu roadside lovemaking, if that. He normally wasn't ready to go again quite so soon, but these were not normal circumstances. Mutilating the captive had fired him up in more ways than one, getting the adrenaline pumping and elevating his heart rate. He felt up for just about anything now, and that definitely included fucking his gorgeous wife again.

An odd idea occurred to him. They could do it right here on the floor in front of the bound man. Give the poor bastard a show before beginning a more severe phase of his torture. Fucking in front of a person they planned to kill would lend the proceedings a decidedly kinkier edge. He was sure Lindsey would be up for it. "Kinky" was a mild word for the shit she was into.

He forced his gaze away from her as she arrived at the second-floor landing and went into one of the rooms up there. Taking a flat-head screwdriver from the toolbox, he grabbed another chair from the table, plopped it down in front of the captive, and sat.

He smiled and leaned forward a bit, bracing his forearms on his knees as he held the screwdriver loosely in his right hand and bounced it up and down. "You know what? I just realized I still don't even know your name. Never thought to ask before you went off to la-la land. Guess it doesn't really matter, huh? Guy like you, you're not even a real person to me. Poor. Non-white. That makes all this a little easier, if I'm being honest. You know what I mean? You told me you work at a supermarket, right? And you're, what, maybe in your mid-thirties?" He shook his head, sneering. "That's some really sad shit there, bucko. Not exactly the ambitious type, are you? Based on that shitty excuse for a car you were driving, I'm betting you don't make much more than minimum wage. My wife and I are both six-figure earners and we're not even in our thirties yet. What do you think of that?"

The bound man said something Grant interpreted as noncommittal, but was indecipherable behind the gag.

He tapped the sharp end of the screwdriver against the man's knee. "I'm sorry, I couldn't quite make that out. Shall I take my wife's panties out of your mouth?"

The question elicited an emphatic nod from the captive.

Grant sighed and shook his head in an expression of mock sadness. Behind the look of fake empathy, however, he was enjoying this opportunity to mentally torment a helpless human being. It filled him with a sense of power unrivaled by anything in his experience. It made him feel god-like. He could do anything at all to this man. *Anything*. He could, if he so chose, free him from his bonds and allow him to escape with no further damage done to his body. Not that he'd ever do anything so stupid, but that wasn't the point. The point was, it was his choice alone to make.

He had the power. Not anyone else.

For now, anyway. Until Lindsey returned, of course.

Still feigning a sadness he doubted even a guy like this was gullible enough to buy into, he said, "I'm afraid I can't do that. I'd rather not listen to you babble and whine like a bitch just yet. Frankly, I'm kind of surprised you don't want my wife's underwear in your mouth. Her snatch is a magical fucking place. I can tell you that for a lock-solid fact, what with all the countless hours I've spent with it on my face. You should feel privileged to have this opportunity, you greasy piece of shit, getting to taste her like that. You're definitely not worthy."

Grant was surprised by the harshness of some of the things coming out of his mouth. They were not things he'd ever say in a normal setting or situation. Moreover, the sentiments expressed didn't reflect any long-withheld private feelings, at least not any he'd been aware of on a conscious level. They almost seemed to come from nowhere, though he realized that couldn't be the case. Perhaps they'd always lurked inside him, these feelings of inherent superiority, hidden away inside one of the nastier dark corners of his psyche. And now the door to that part of him had been unlocked by participating in the degradation of this man. It made as much sense as anything else, he supposed.

He stood up and moved a step closer, pressing the end of the screwdriver into the man's cheek, dimpling the flesh. The bound man started shaking and whimpering again, breathing hard behind the gag. "How about this idea as an alternative in the meantime?" He pressed the head of the screwdriver harder against the man's cheek, dimpling the flesh even more. Any harder and he'd probably draw blood. "How about I make a hole in your face with this screwdriver?" He laughed. "That'd help, right? An extra airway to make your breathing easier?"

Grant increased the pressure he was applying with the screwdriver. A bead of blood appeared and began to slide down the man's cheek. The captive whined and started panting heavily. He sounded like he was on the verge of hyperventilating. After allowing the man another few moments to exist in that state of heightened panic, he took the screwdriver away and laughed.

"Wow!" he said, laughing yet again and shaking his head. "I'm getting a way bigger kick out of this torture thing than I ever imagined. Really thought I wouldn't be into this part of it at all, but it's so addicting, this feeling of power. It's like how I imagine junkies feel when they take that first hit of crack or meth or whatever. You should try it sometime." He fake-winced as he said this, but there was still an edge of a smile in the expression. "Oh, wait. You can't. You won't ever get the chance because you're not leaving this place alive. I mean, you know that, right?"

Tears leaked from the corners of the man's eyes as he began to sob miserably, his chin dipping toward his chest.

Grant grabbed a fistful of the man's black hair and jerked his head up straight. He held the tip of the screwdriver a small fraction of an inch away from one of his eyes. "Stop that blubbering," he said, shifting to a tone far more menacing than what he'd utilized before. "Look at you. Crying like a fucking baby. No real man does that. Then again, you're not a real man at all, are you? A real man would never allow himself to get taken like that by a woman. Do you have even an ounce of self-respect left? I don't think you do."

He gave that fistful of hair a slow, hard twist, drawing forth another loud whine of pain.

"God, I love that fucking sound!"

He relinquished his grip on the man's hair and after a moment the sound abated. Sitting down again, Grant allowed the man some moments to calm down. Then, just as soon as the whining had ceased entirely and his breathing evened out, he leaned forward again, raised the screwdriver up high, and slammed it down.

The captive screamed with even more unhinged ferocity than before as the sharp end of the screwdriver punched into his leg just above the knee. He tilted his head back and put the full force of his lungs into it, screaming over and over with everything he had.

Grant tightened his grip on the handle and clapped his other hand around it for additional force as he gritted his teeth and worked hard at driving the length of steel deeper into the man's leg. By the time he stopped, barely more than an inch of steel remained visible between the handle and the captive's bloodsoaked jeans.

Letting go of the handle at last, he leaned back in his chair and spent some time admiring his bloody handiwork. The man continued screaming and moaning for a considerable period of time.

Grant smiled at him with his arms folded contentedly across his chest. In a few more moments, however, his smile began to slip. He turned his head and glanced up at the second-floor loft. No sign of Lindsey.

He looked at the captive and frowned. "Huh. She's been up there a while. I should probably go check on her. I'll be right back, so don't go anywhere."

He gripped the screwdriver's handle and gave it another twist for good measure, resulting in the expected vocalization of profound agony. After having a good chuckle over this, Grant got to his feet and went upstairs.

11

THE WHITE MAN WAS GONE by the time the pain relented enough for Jorge Mendez to open his eyes again. He was still in agony, but now it was at a level where there was room in his mind—just barely—for contemplation of other things, a state of affairs he knew would be short-lived if he couldn't figure out how to get out of this mess.

They were just getting started on him. These were the early stages of a process the demented couple planned to draw out for hours, perhaps all through the night and into tomorrow. They hadn't explicitly spelled it out that way, but he'd pieced enough together from the things they'd said to know this was the case. His abduction at the roadside clearing was a thing that'd come about by chance, but this was a planned event in their lives. If it wasn't him sitting in this chair, it'd be someone else. It'd been his rotten luck to happen along and have a vehicular breakdown at the exact wrong time.

His father used to say the family was living under a curse and had been for generations. Jorge wasn't a believer in such things, but it was true there was plentiful evidence of bad luck hounding the Mendez clan down through the years. His grandfather was killed by a hit-and-run driver who was never caught one day after retiring from the police force. Two younger siblings serving in the military were killed in separate incidents in Iraq and Afghanistan. An uncle he was close to accidentally killed himself while cleaning his gun. A young nephew disappeared one summer day a decade ago and was never found. And that was just scratching the surface. There were numerous other examples of the "curse" taking a heavy toll on the family, and now it was looking like he'd soon fall victim to it, as well.

Jorge wasn't quite ready to give up yet, however, even though the situation appeared bleak verging on completely hopeless. This was the first time he'd been left alone in the room since regaining consciousness. Any small remaining sliver of hope hinged on what he did in these next few moments. There wasn't even the slightest bit of give to his bonds, though. Every attempt to move his limbs was an exercise in extreme frustration. That bitch had been devilishly thorough in securing him to the chair. He felt frozen in place.

Clearly any effort to twist or wriggle free was doomed to failure, unless he was able to change some other aspect of the equation. He thought of all the old TV shows and movies he'd seen in which people in situations like this were able to get free by causing the chair to topple over and break. Given the sturdiness of this chair and the elaborate bindings, he doubted this would work in his case, but he didn't know what else he could do. He had to give it a shot. The only other option was to sit here and do nothing while he cried and moaned and thought about how he was probably never going to see any of his family or friends again.

He started trying to rock the chair side-to-side and at first was only able to make the chair legs lift a fraction of an inch off the floor. Just as he was about to bear down harder and redouble the effort, he stopped entirely, hearing raised voices from upstairs. He couldn't quite make out what was being said, but the man sounded angry while there was more than a hint of defensiveness in the woman's voice. He spent a moment wondering whether it was a good or bad thing for him that they were fighting. Could go either way, he guessed. At the very least, they were occupied with something else for now. Meanwhile, he needed to ignore them and focus entirely on the task at hand.

Maybe rocking the chair side-to-side wasn't the best idea. He imagined it toppling sideways and falling flat on the floor with no damage done to its structure. Might be better to make the thing fall over at an angle. More of a chance of causing one of the chair's legs to snap and break that way, he figured. In any case, he had to work as quickly as possible, because he doubted whatever disagreement they were having up there would keep them occupied for long.

His plan was far from perfect, of course. It was hard to imagine, for instance, how he might get free of even a broken chair with so much duct tape wrapped around his limbs, but that was no excuse for not trying.

He began trying to rock the chair backward with the intent of throwing his weight in such a way that would cause it to fall at an angle at the right moment. At first this was even harder than trying to rock the chair side-to-side. He couldn't get the legs to lift off the floor at all. The couple was still fighting upstairs and so far had given no indication of hearing what he was up to. He redoubled the effort, putting everything he had into it. Finally, the front legs of the chair began to lift off the floor. What felt like maybe a mere millimeter the first time and then maybe a full inch the next.

A spark of hope ignited inside him. Maybe he really could get this done with a bit of luck. Screw that family curse bullshit. He was getting out of here and back home to his dog. The chair almost went over the next time he rocked it backward. He was sure the next time would do it.

He rocked the chair backward yet again and just as it was finally starting to topple over, he began to perceive an unexpected sound.

An engine.

A vehicle of some sort was coming up the long drive to the cabin.

12

UP HERE ON THE SECOND floor, there were two bedrooms and a bathroom at the far end of the loft. Lindsey decided to check the bathroom first for the simple reason that she needed to pee. While sitting on the can, she spent some time looking at her phone and scrolling through her various social media feeds. None of it was all that interesting, the usual political screeds and self-absorbed crap from the usual vapid people. She hit the like button on a few of the usual things her friends and followers would expect her to like, but even this she didn't give much of a shit about. It was habit.

Much more interesting developments were occurring downstairs and she was eager to get back in the thick of things. She smiled when she heard the man she'd taken screaming in pain again. These were his loudest screams yet. Even up here, the volume was ear-piercing. This made her happy. Grant was finally really getting into the spirit of the thing, tapping that sadistic potential she'd always suspected was there.

She wiped and flushed then pulled up her shorts as she got up from the toilet. Tucking her phone away in a back pocket, she washed her hands at the basin and dried them on a small hand towel hanging from a rack. A larger bath towel was hanging from a hook on the back of the door, but there was no linen closet in here. She'd need to search the bedrooms next, but instead of immediately doing that, she lingered inside the bathroom door and listened a moment longer as Grant continued to torment the captive. She couldn't make out every word he was saying, but she heard enough to realize her husband was so into what he was doing he likely wouldn't miss her for at least a few minutes longer.

The surge of arousal she'd experienced while torturing the Mexican, or whatever he was, was still with her, albeit faded slightly. It increased again when it occurred to her she could take a private moment to look at the secret digital photo album on her phone while Grant was otherwise occupied.

Easing the bathroom door closed without fully pushing it shut, she took the phone from her pocket and backtracked until her butt was braced against the edge of the basin. The photo album app was designed to look like an online banking portal. When a password was entered, however, it was revealed as something else altogether—a means of storing photos the user didn't want others to see.

She bit her bottom lip and squirmed slightly against the edge of the basin, quickly becoming aroused again as she scrolled through the dozens of steamy pictures from her wild night with Justin and Kurt. Many of them were rapidly taken shots of Justin ferociously banging her from behind in her own bedroom. These showed her with her eyes screwed shut and her mouth open wide as she screamed in ecstasy and clutched at the rumpled bed sheets. There were pictures of Justin and Kurt doing things to each other, but these she found less interesting. All had been taken the night of Grant's bachelor party, when he'd stayed out late drinking with his work buddies.

One picture in particular was her special favorite. She was in her wedding dress and a nude Justin was positioned above her in the bed with his cock rammed down her throat. His sculpted physique was truly something to behold. He was like one of those old Greek statues come to life, only even more impressively muscled. Moaning softly, she pushed a hand down the front of her shorts and started rubbing her clit, slowly at first, then with rapidly increasing intensity.

She was so into it the creaking of the door didn't register as Grant pushed it open and came into the bathroom. By the time she sensed his presence, he was already several steps into the room and hiding what she was doing was not possible. In desperation, she tried tucking the phone away in a back pocket of her shorts, but he snatched it away from her before she could do that. She screamed at him and tried to snatch it back, but he backhanded her and sent her sprawling in an awkward heap to the floor. When she tried to get back to her feet, he kicked her in the stomach hard enough to blast the air from her lungs and leave her temporarily immobilized.

Looking up at him through eyes bleary with tears, she curled into a fetal ball and clutched at her aching stomach. She was stunned by the savagery of the assault. Never in a million years would she have guessed Grant capable of assaulting her so violently. Even through her tears, she could see her husband's rage building as he stared at the image on her phone, his face twitching and turning red as the hand gripping the phone trembled from the mounting fury. He looked like he was about to blow a gasket by the time he finished scrolling through her formerly secret photos. She wished she could rewind time a few minutes and resist the temptation to look at them.

When he looked at her again, it was like looking into the face of a stranger. There was murder in those glaring eyes. She sensed it as clearly as she'd ever sensed anything. If she didn't do something to defuse the situation right now, the guy tied to the chair downstairs wouldn't be the only one who'd die in this cabin tonight. "Grant, honey . . ." She sniffled and choked back a sob. "I can explain. If you'd just listen . . ."

"You fucking worthless whore!" The muscles in his neck stood out in stark relief as he roared and raged at her. He turned the phone around and put the screen up close to her face as he knelt in front of her. "How long have you been fucking my faggot cousin behind my back, you dirty fucking cunt!?"

He grabbed her by the throat and throttled her, making the back of her head bounce off the floor. She clawed at his hand with her long nails, drawing blood but failing to budge it even an iota. All the while, he continued to roar at her. Her head was throbbing and she was starting to feel queasy, bile rising in her throat. Spittle flew in her face as he screamed at her. In those moments, he looked more like an uncaged wild animal than a human being.

With a hard flick of his hand, he sent her phone sailing across the room. She heard it smack the wall and fall into the tub. Now he had both hands wrapped around her throat and was still increasing the pressure. Her vision turned blurry and she knew she was moments away from dying if she couldn't make him stop somehow.

She knew there'd been an element of risk in what she'd done with Justin and his boyfriend. Even arrogance. When doing a thing like that, there was always a chance of getting caught, especially when one kept photographic evidence of the transgression. Yet she'd never truly believed it would happen. She'd believed her husband too easily pliable and oblivious, and she'd been completely confident in her ability to deflect his suspicions should any ever arise. His initial meekness in dealing with their captive had only reinforced this belief. She'd believed she could get away with anything. About that, she'd clearly been wrong to a horrifying degree. She'd been wrong about so many things. By goading him into hurting the man downstairs, she'd awakened within him a capacity for violence, possibly sealing her own fate.

Summoning the last of her fading strength, she reached up and jabbed a long thumbnail into a bulging eye. That did the trick. His hands came away from her throat as he stood up and reeled backward, clapping a hand over his injured eye. He stumbled and crashed into the wash basin, cracking his lower back against its edge. He cried out again and dropped to his knees. In the same instant, Lindsey rolled onto her side and tried pushing herself into a sitting position. Her breath wheezed as she struggled to draw in air.

The relief she felt at having staved off imminent death was immense but was tempered with the knowledge that she was far from out of danger. Grant was already getting back to his feet before she was able to sit up. Rolling toward him, she grabbed him by the ankle of his left foot and yanked as hard as she could. His feet came out from under him and he pitched backward again. He shrieked in pain as his back again crashed against the basin and he dropped to the floor.

He was moaning and writhing around weakly on the floor as Lindsey at last managed to stand up. She stared down at her husband and spent several seconds mired in indecision about what to do. He was at least temporarily incapacitated, albeit not unconscious. Her instinct was to run. Take the keys, get in the truck, and speed away from here.

The wheels in her head were spinning as she weighed all the angles. She could go to the police and report the assault, have Grant's wife-beating ass hauled off to jail, but that would require having to finish off the captive on her way out the door. Dead men tell no tales, after all. She'd also have to arrange the scene in a way that would throw the weight of suspicion on Grant. She could portray him as an unhinged maniac who snatched the brown-skinned stranger off the street for racist reasons. At the same time, she could paint a picture of herself as a victim, too, a woman terrorized into staying with him while he tortured and murdered that poor, unfortunate man.

The upside of this approach was it would eventually allow her to wipe her hands more or less clean of this clusterfuck and return to something resembling her normal life. She'd have to start over again in a lot of ways, of course, but it'd be worth it in the end. No longer bound to a man who'd harbored a hidden and shocking capacity for explosive levels of jealous rage, she'd be free to search for a new long-term lover. She might eventually find someone even better for her than she'd falsely imagined Grant would be.

Or she could go another direction entirely, try a lone-wolf kind of thing for a while. There might be a lot fewer complications that way if she decided to pursue an ongoing career in murder. Almost as soon as this occurred to her, she knew it was what she wanted. That freedom to live whatever way she wished and kill whenever she felt like it. For so long she'd lived a life constrained by concerns about the necessity of presenting an image of normality to the world. She'd always believed marriage was an integral part of that. Maybe she'd been completely wrong about all of it all along. She saw now there was no good reason she couldn't do whatever she wanted without a constant male companion by her side. Never mind what she'd told Grant earlier—for the first time in her life, she would be truly, completely free.

All these considerations flashed through her head in a span of mere seconds. Grant was still down there on the floor, writhing and moaning, but that might not remain the case much longer. His moans were louder and he was squirming around with a little more vigor. Allowing him more time to recover would be a mistake.

She glanced around the bathroom, looking for something good to use as a weapon. She smiled when her gaze landed on the toilet tank. The heavy porcelain lid would work nicely as a tool for bashing in Grant's skull. Before she could take a step in that direction, a pair of unexpected sounds stopped her in her tracks.

There was a crash from downstairs. She could think of only one explanation for that. The bound man had managed to topple the chair over. Even if he managed to partially shatter the chair by doing that, she doubted he'd be able to get free, at least not without many more minutes of unimpeded struggling. His elaborate bindings would slow him down considerably, giving her more than enough time to kill Grant and then get back downstairs and finish off the captive.

She took a first step toward the toilet.

And then, a second later, she at last perceived the sound of an engine coming up the drive toward the cabin. Again, she stopped in her tracks. She felt her heart stutter as a jolt of alarm flashed through her.

Grant was sitting up by then, staring blearily at her and wincing from the pain of his injuries. "You hear that, too, right?"

"Yeah. Shit."

There was a moment of intense eye contact between them.

Then Lindsey let out a big breath and held out a hand. "Truce?"

Grant sighed and nodded. "Truce."

He reached out and gripped her extended hand, allowing her to help him to his feet. There was another of those moments of sustained, intense eye contact as they listened to the sound of the engine getting louder and louder. The loud rumbling went on another moment.

Then the engine cut off. Moments later, the front door creaked open and someone entered the cabin.

Grant and Lindsey nodded at each other. Then they raced out of the bathroom and hurried downstairs.

13

PIERCE WEATHERBY MAINTAINED A DEATH grip on the minivan's steering wheel the entire way up the narrow and winding private drive to the old family cabin. Even with his brights on, it was often barely possible to tell where the edges of the drive gave way to the perilously steep drop-offs to either side. For the life of him, he'd never understand why guardrails had never been installed to reduce the possibility of some calamitous accident.

He'd always found the journey up the narrow drive at least somewhat unnerving, but it'd never been so outright scary as now. The reason for the disparity was simple—all those other times he'd driven up to the cabin in broad daylight. In daylight, it wasn't too bad so long as one paid close attention to what one was doing. Perhaps foolishly, he'd thought it would be much the same at night, his familiarity with the terrain making up for the lack of abundant sunshine. It'd been a long time since he'd been so egregiously wrong about anything.

The worst part about it was he had no one to blame but himself.

The idea for the impromptu trip had been his own. Given the chance to do it again, he'd still think the trip was a good idea, but he'd probably delay their departure until early the following day. Instead he'd made an impetuous, perhaps foolish decision to leave late in the day in the midst of a moment of stress.

He'd spent the bulk of the day listening to his family squabble over a range of the pettiest things imaginable. Mostly it was the kids, but Piper, his wife of twenty-odd years now, had gotten in her fair share of verbal sniping as well. Some of it was directed at the kids, but quite a bit of it had been directed at him. This was nothing new, but it'd been getting steadily worse over the last several weeks, ever since the beginning of August, when he'd taken early retirement from the highly successful company he'd founded over a decade ago.

He understood it.

They weren't used to having him around all the time. In the past, even when he wasn't busy at the office, he was away traveling on business. He was often gone for a week or more at a time. By putting an abrupt and total end to all that, he'd disrupted long-established routines for all of them.

In particular, the kids had enjoyed a level of autonomy not common among their peers. As long as they weren't out getting into trouble—and that had never been a serious issue with either of them—they were allowed to do pretty much as they pleased. This state of affairs was mostly their mother's doing. Being away as much as he'd been, it'd been only practical to leave the establishment of household rules and child-raising responsibilities up to her. He'd never had an issue with this until he was suddenly home all the time and discovered how lax she'd been with them. As best he could tell, there'd been no real rules at all. After getting out of school each day, the kids were often away from home until long after dark, often not getting back from wherever they'd been until nearly midnight.

Pierce found this alarming.

Nearly as upsetting was a separate but related revelation. He soon came to understand his wife was rarely around during his former work hours. It didn't take long to realize this wasn't because she was spending time with the kids. If they weren't at school, they were always off doing their own thing and had no interest in spending their leisure time hanging out with Mom. Her daily absence during those hours was something he'd never noticed, but once he started staying home all the time, it became too glaring a thing to miss.

When he quizzed her about it, she gave vague answers about being out shopping, getting lunch with "the ladies", or trips to the gym. He knew she had a gym membership and lady friends he knew next-to-nothing about, so these were valid reasons for being away from home. Even taken all together, however, did they really account for being gone eight to ten hours a day every damn day? He didn't think so, but when he pressed her on the matter, she got defensive about it in the extreme. Lately she'd started calling him selfish for taking early retirement, but she wasn't the only one mad about the new way of things. He'd recently instituted a new rule for the kids—be home no later than nine o'clock every school night, eleven o'clock on Fridays and Saturdays. Non-compliance would mean the suspension of their generous weekly allowances.

The result? Everyone was mad at him now.

And today had been the worst day yet. Piper and the kids kept bitching at him nonstop about this and that. They yelled and snapped at each other, too. It gave Pierce a headache he didn't think would ever go away. They kept at it until he lost his cool and screamed at them loud enough to force a rare moment of blessed silence.

Then it came to him. His brilliant goddamned idea. Only now it seemed considerably less brilliant than it had at conception. He decided they needed to get away from it all for a few days. Out of the city and off to the mountains. Out to the old cabin they hadn't visited in a while. He still had the keys he'd used the last time, having failed to return them to Carl Weatherby Jr., one of the rotating collective of elder Weatherbys who took it upon themselves to look after and maintain the place. Carl had kept after him to return the keys for a while, but in those days Pierce had little time to trouble himself with what he considered trivialities. He was a busy man with a lot of responsibilities, after all. After a while, old Carl stopped calling and leaving messages, and not too long ago he'd learned of Carl's passing.

The keys were his now, as far as he was concerned, and he could make use of them whenever he wished. And today he wished to do precisely that. The fervency of this wish had waned some in the hours since hustling his family into the minivan after hurriedly packing up a couple days' worth of clothes and supplies. He'd pitched it to them as an opportunity for a rare family adventure, a break from their daily norms. It would be a good thing for all of them. And, after all, it'd only be a couple of days. After that, they'd be allowed to return to their usual self-centered ways. Only maybe—just *maybe*—it'd be with a new and improved attitude toward, well, everything following their bonding experience in the mountains.

The kids had warmed to the idea after some initial grumbling. It helped that he'd promised to upgrade their phones upon their return home. Of them all, it was Piper who seemed to harbor the most resentment about being made to come along. She'd been short with him several times during the drive and kept giving him sharp looks. By now he was about fifty-percent convinced she was having an affair with some unknown man. Maybe more than fifty percent. It would explain a lot.

Pierce hit the brake when he realized he'd allowed the minivan to drift dangerously close to the drop-off on the left-hand side of the drive. "Shit!"

Piper's nose crinkled as she made a sound of disdain. "Oh, perfect. You're going to plunge us to our deaths before we even get to the damn cabin."

Pierce squeezed his eyes shut and kept them that way a moment as he gritted his teeth. He was striving to find a calm center somewhere inside him, but it wasn't easy with the way his wife was constantly harping at him.

She kept at it.

"Honestly, I'm astonished by your rapid descent into total incompetence. Is that the real reason you retired, honey? You sensed an early onset of dementia and decided to get out while the getting was good, before it could get worse and you started embarrassing yourself by pissing your trousers in board meetings?"

Kelsey, their seventeen-year-old daughter, giggled at this remark.

Her fifteen-year-old brother, Rory, gasped in apparent shock, although Pierce thought he detected a slight tinge of mockery in the sound.

Pierce let out a breath and opened his eyes. He glanced at his wife, a wounded look on his face. "At this point, I'm starting to think I'd be doing us all a favor by taking a suicide plunge off the fucking ridge. This family is almost terminally dysfunctional."

Piper guffawed and rolled her eyes. "Oh, please. You love yourself too much to do that."

He glared at her a moment longer, then his expression softened and he laughed. "You're right. I do. Love the kids, too. You, though . . ."

He trailed off, letting the obvious implication linger as an uncomfortable silence stretched out inside the minivan. Pierce made eye contact with his wife and this time he saw some hurt in her expression. He derived a nasty sort of satisfaction from seeing this. It made him feel dirty and mean. He didn't like that at all, didn't like to think he was that sort of person.

His wife had tears in her eyes. She sniffled and wiped them away.

He sighed. "Piper, I'm sorry. I'm just really stressed, that's all."

Kelsey harrumphed in the back seat. "Worst. Dad. Ever."

Pierce was mentally scrambling for a way to defuse the situation. He was on the brink of ruining the trip already, and they weren't even all the way up to the cabin yet. He was going to need a stiff drink when they got there. Maybe a few of them. He was on the verge of opening his mouth to spew more emptily placating words when the baby stirred and cried softly in his sleep.

Pierce twisted around and peered through the gap between seats. One-year-old Vance Weatherby was strapped into his car seat between his much older siblings. He'd been blessedly quiet for much of the trip, but that couldn't last forever.

Kelsey looked up from her phone and sneered at him. "Oh, great, you've awakened the squalling beast."

Pierce yearned to snap something at the girl for being so disrespectful, but he held his tongue, not wishing to further inflame the situation, which was already hovering on the brink of disaster. He stared at the baby a moment longer and faced forward when it didn't cry out again.

He nudged the steering wheel to the right and got the minivan rolling again. No one said anything the rest of the way up the drive, not until they were approaching the last bend in the road and the top of the cabin became visible through the trees ringing the larger piece of land at the end of the ridge.

Piper cleared her throat. "Fuck this. We're going back home first thing in the morning. When we get there, I'm calling a lawyer to initiate divorce proceedings."

More gasps from the back of the van.

This time there was no hint of mockery in the sound.

Pierce was too temporarily stunned by his wife's unexpected pronouncement to respond to it. His throat felt tight and something clenched in his chest. A wave of powerful emotion swept through him and now there were tears in his eyes. He felt helpless. Powerless. His family was abruptly falling apart and he felt incapable of saving it. He knew he didn't want to lose them, even his probably unfaithful wife, and he also knew he would soon be begging her to change her mind.

Before he could do that, however, the minivan came around that last bend and the cabin came into full view.

Rory leaned forward from the back and poked his head between the front seats. "Hey, somebody's already here."

Pierce frowned as he guided the minivan closer to the cabin. "I see that. Get back, please."

Rory ignored his father and leaned forward a bit more. "That truck looks old and creepy. Great, Dad. I think you've taken us into an *Evil Dead* or *Texas Chainsaw*-type situation. We'll be dead at the hands of some backwoods hicks soon."

Pierce gave his son a little push to make him return to his seat and said, "Don't be so dramatic. The gate was locked. This has to be someone we know."

Piper grunted. "That truck does look kind of familiar. I can't quite place it." She glanced at her husband, her face again registering deep disdain. "You did check to see if the cabin was being used this weekend before dragging us out here, didn't you? I mean, even you couldn't possibly be that fucking stupid. Could you?"

A surge of anger swelled inside Pierce, but he pushed it back, still determined not to let it get the better of him. It was true he hadn't gotten in touch with one of the geezers who took care of the place, but he didn't want to admit the oversight. He'd be derided for it mercilessly by all of them and he didn't think he could handle that.

After pulling the minivan up alongside the truck and its attached camper, he put it in park and cut the engine, taking the keys from the ignition slot. "Sit tight here. I'm gonna check things out."

Piper rolled her eyes and groaned. "It's not worth it. Someone is clearly using the goddamn cabin. You should turn this thing around and take us the fuck back home. And after that, you can check yourself into a hotel."

Pierce ignored that as he unbuckled his seatbelt and opened the door. "This shouldn't take but a minute. Whoever this is might even let us stay the night at least. There's plenty of room inside."

He climbed out of the minivan, dropped the keys in his hip pocket, and started walking up toward the cabin even as his wife continued to yell at him. As he began to mount the steps to the porch, he heard a heavy thump from somewhere behind the cabin's closed front door. It sounded as if someone had fallen to the floor, which was alarming. Maybe it was one of the old Weatherby guys, and he'd had a heart attack.

Moving faster now, he went to the door and tested the knob. It was unlocked and turned easily in his hand. He pushed the door open and hurriedly entered the cabin, determined to offer help if one of those old guys needed it. This was in part driven by genuine concern for the well-being of one of his rarely seen elder relatives. There was also a part of him, however, that relished the opportunity to play the role of hero in front of his family. He wasn't anything like an EMT by any means, but he had basic CPR skills. It was within the possibility he could save a life.

He stopped in his tracks once he was fully inside the cabin, taken aback by the shocking sight that greeted him. A brown-skinned man was bound to a chair that had toppled over and was now on its side on the floor. In addition to his bonds, he had silver strips of duct tape over his mouth and presumably a gag of some kind behind the tape. The man's eyes bugged out when he saw Pierce. He frantically attempted to tell him something that was indecipherable because of the tape.

Completely mystified by what was going on here—but knowing it could be nothing good—Pierce inched carefully closer to the bound man. He felt a queasy twinge in his gut when he saw the screwdriver protruding from the man's leg. A closer look revealed that someone had snipped off pieces of the man's ears.

Pierce put a hand to his mouth. "Jesus."

He was torn between still wanting to offer the man assistance and the option of backing out of this situation and getting far away from here as quickly as possible. The one thing that was absolutely undeniable was that something very bad was happening here. Something actively dangerous.

He took a first step backward, knees shaking precariously as fear began to overcome him. Whatever brand of madness was going on here, he couldn't let his family be exposed to it. He took another shaky step backward and now the man on the floor was whining behind his gag. His desperation was obvious and Pierce did feel bad about abandoning the man to his fate, but his family's safety was the priority here.

"I'm sorry, buddy," he said softly, still hoping to avoid detection by whoever had done this horrible thing. "I'm getting out of here, but I'll call the cops as soon as I'm on my way."

He started to turn toward the door and that was when he heard the pounding footsteps. Glancing up, he saw a young couple charging toward the wooden staircase at the far end of the second-floor loft. The woman was a stranger, but he recognized the man as a younger cousin from his side of the family. He was a Weatherby. Grant, that was his name. The woman was blond and long-legged, highly attractive. She reminded him strongly of a younger version of Piper, a well-bred rich girl. He didn't notice she looked like she'd been smacked around until the couple came galloping down the stairs into the main room.

Pierce was so surprised by this development he halted his retreat to the open front door, his face twisting into a deep frown as the woman veered toward the table in the dining area while Grant approached him with a strained smile on his face.

He also looked like he'd taken a bit of a beating.

Pierce held up a hand, palm turned outward. "Whoa there, kid. It's Grant, right?"

His handsome young cousin nodded, smiling broadly in a way

that might have been disarming under other circumstances. "Sure is. And you're Pierce, right?"

Pierce nodded slowly. "Yep. You mind explaining why you have a tied-up Mexican on your floor? This doesn't look good."

Grant grimaced and scratched the side of his neck. "That's a long story, but there's a good explanation. This guy broke in, you see. He was going to rob us and kill us, but we, uh . . . managed to subdue him."

The tied-up man made an emphatic noise behind his gag that sounded very much like he was saying, "Bullshit."

Pierce made a contemplative sound. "Uh-huh. Why does he have a screwdriver poking out of his leg?"

Grant frowned. "Um . . ."

He trailed off, unable, apparently, to elaborate further.

By then his good-looking female companion had sidled up next to him. She had a hand behind her back, which Pierce found more than a little worrisome. He hadn't kept an eye on her while talking to Grant, but now he suspected she was hiding some kind of weapon. Now he shifted his weight from one side to the other, preparing to make a mad dash for the door. Blood relation or not, it was clear Grant was up to some especially vile form of villainy here. Something for which there could be no good or understandable explanation.

The woman came a step closer, still keeping that hand hidden behind her back. "You need to understand what really happened here, mister." She smiled in a sexily distracting way, swaying her hips slightly as she came still another step closer. "It's absolutely not what it looks like. This bad hombre tried to rape me, but he couldn't get it up. He beat the shit out of me out of frustration. Beat the shit out of Grant, too, before we got the better of him. And, well, I know it's wrong and all, but we were so upset. We decided to get a little revenge on him. You understand, right?"

Pierce shook his head. "I'm not at all sure I do, young lady. Why don't you show me what you're hiding behind your back before you come any closer?"

Her smile had a distinctly nasty edge to it now. "Afraid I can't do that, gramps."

Pierce was about to retort when he heard a creaking sound from the porch behind him.

Then he heard his daughter meekly say, "Daddy? Is everything all right in there?"

Instinct caused him to start turning in her direction.

In the same instant, the woman came rushing toward him and slammed the big blade of a hunting knife deep into his stomach.

Out on the porch, Kelsey screamed.

14

LINDSEY RIPPED THE HUNTING KNIFE out of Pierce's stomach and immediately rammed it back in again, this time higher up, closer to his sternum. The knife only went in about halfway this second time before striking bone. She tried pulling it back out again but was forced to work harder at it this time because it was embedded in something, bone or tough muscle tissue. She screeched in frustration as Pierce screamed and flailed at her.

The knife finally came out again and Lindsey directed her next thrust of the blade at his throat. Miraculously still on his feet, Pierce flinched away at the last second. Instead of a direct plunge deep into the center of his throat, the blade skidded along the side of his neck. The blade nonetheless sliced deep enough to cause bright red blood to repeatedly spurt out of the new hole in his flesh. Grant had a feeling the blade had nicked one of the big, super-important neck arteries. His uncle clamped a hand over the wound, but without the immediate assistance of a medical professional, he was probably doomed already.

Grant had mixed feelings about that. In truth, he had mixed feelings about a lot of things. The image of a perfect relationship with Lindsey had been shattered, revealed as little more than a hollow, empty lie. He'd loved her completely and unconditionally from the start, had barely even given other women a second look since getting involved with her. She'd always swore she felt the same way about him, but all along she'd been fucking other people behind his back.

The sickening images of all the things she'd done with his cousin and his cousin's flamer boyfriend were seared into his brain. He had no doubt there'd been many other secretive trysts along the way. She'd made a fool of him and in a flash of instinctive, blinding rage he'd tried to murder her. There could be no coming back from that shit for either of them. Not now. Not ever.

And now, after having shown up out of the absolute fucking blue, a family member was dying right in front of him. He hadn't seen Pierce in a long time, probably well over a decade. They were cousins, but the age difference was such that Grant had always thought of him as more of an uncle. Though they'd never been close, he remembered liking the guy well enough. He'd always treated him well at those old family gatherings, never seeming to look down on him because he was younger. Being involved in his murder, even in the role of a bystander, made him feel kind of shitty, but there was no other choice to be made here. Lindsey had understood that immediately and was taking care of business while he stood here and watched with his mouth hanging open.

To further complicate matters, Pierce had not come alone. That voice out there on the porch wasn't one he recognized, but it clearly belonged to a young person. His daughter, probably. Grant's stomach knotted painfully as he realized what would have to happen next. This whole situation was spiraling rapidly out of control. His only hope now was that no one else had accompanied Pierce on his trip up to the cabin.

Pierce lurched away from Lindsey and staggered as he began to turn about, his hand still clamped to the spurting neck wound as he made it a few feet closer to the door before collapsing. He hit the floor with a heavy thump and didn't move again.

Through the open door, Grant saw the girl standing out there on the porch with a stricken look on her face. She was young and pretty, somewhere in her late teens, probably. He'd seen her before, he realized, but she'd been a small child then. The cell phone held loosely in her trembling fingers slipped from her grip and landed with a clatter on the porch. She stared at her father's unmoving body and screamed. Her gaze shifted to Lindsey and she screamed again.

Lindsey's head snapped toward Grant. "Get that bitch! Now!"

Grant glanced at his wife.

Her face and the front of her shirt were covered in blood. The savage twist of those blood-spattered features made her look like a raving lunatic. She screamed at him when he did not instantly obey her command. The sound was so ear-splittingly shrill and filled with such apocalyptic fury it compelled him to action.

He started moving quickly toward the door.

The girl shrieked in fright.

She turned and ran.

Grant picked up the pace and ran after her, following her down the steps and out into the clearing in front of the cabin. She gave the camper a wide berth and headed for a steel-blue minivan parked near it. The sick feeling in Grant's gut worsened as he discerned dim shapes of other people inside the minivan. Doors on the vehicle opened when the girl neared it, but by then he'd about caught up to her. He heard voices calling out to her from inside the vehicle. The voices were tinged with alarm and confusion, but they did not communicate actual terror quite yet.

That was about to change.

The first scream to emanate from the minivan came immediately after he summoned an extra reserve of strength and leaped forward to tackle the girl. He hit her square in the back and she instantly collapsed beneath him as he drove her hard to the ground. She screamed and squirmed beneath him, but because she was face-down on the ground, he was able to easily hold her in place. How long that might last was another question entirely. Without assistance, he wouldn't be able to keep her pinned down indefinitely. Even if she wasn't able to get loose, at some point these other people would come to her aid. He couldn't hold off all of them. He wasn't Superman, after all.

Almost immediately after this thought flashed through his mind, he felt someone kicking him in the side while screaming at him to get off the girl. Actually, what she was repeatedly screaming was, "Get off my daughter!"

So this was Pierce's wife. The girl's mother.

He couldn't remember the woman's name but recalled liking her considerably less than Pierce. She'd come off as cold and snooty back in the day. Sexy, though. He dimly recalled her featuring in some of his masturbation fantasies back then.

He heard another voice. Some other kid. A boy, from the sound of it.

Then the cry of a baby stirring from sleep.

Fuck.

Did these old assholes have a fucking newborn, too? He would've thought the wife was too long in the tooth to still be birthing children at this point. Bitch had to be at least forty.

The kicks to his side landed harder and harder, the girl's mother becoming more frantic and determined to dislodge him by the moment. He was on the verge of attempting to grab her by an ankle when he heard a soft *pop*. She kicked him one more time and then stopped. Seconds later, he heard her drop to the ground a few feet away. The boy shrieked, but did not immediately run away or rush over to help his fallen mother. From the sound of it, he was struggling with something inside the car. The baby's cries grew louder.

Grant twisted his head around for a better look at what was happening. The first thing he saw was the mother's glazed eyes staring blankly at him from where she'd dropped to the ground. A feathered tranquilizer dart protruded from her slender neck. His gaze went higher and he saw the boy leaning into the minivan's back seat through the open door. Grant hoped like hell he wasn't trying to dig a hidden gun out of a glove compartment or travel bag. That would spell instant disaster, assuming the kid could summon the nerve to shoot his family's assailants.

Meanwhile, the girl was still struggling ferociously beneath him. She was screaming at him in a way that communicated terror and defiance, spewing profanities and promising to kill him as soon as she got the chance. The crux of his most pressing problem was simple—he couldn't go after the boy without letting the girl up, at which point she'd become a thousand times more dangerous. He could think of only one solution.

He had to kill the girl.

The thought made him queasy. Standing aside while Lindsey murdered Pierce was one thing. That had been bad enough. The prospect of killing another blood relation with his bare hands made him almost physically sick. She was a total innocent, barely more than a child. Her only crime was being in the wrong place at the wrong time.

No part of him wanted to do it, but the brutal reality of the situation was simple. Any slim chance he still had of returning to his normal life was dependent on the girl dying. With a continually deepening sense of horror, it hit him that they'd all have to die. The girl, the mother, the boy, even the baby. The whole fucking family. He felt like screaming as the sheer enormity of it swept over him. This was a genuine atrocity he was contemplating. The kind of thing monsters did.

He hated it with every fiber of his being.

But it had to be done.

He searched the ground nearby for a rock of ample size, one with enough heft to it to efficiently bash in her skull. There was no sign of anything nearly large enough, only pebbles. Contemplating alternative approaches, he imagined simply snapping her neck. He saw that done in movies a lot and it always looked so easy. He doubted that would be the case in real life, at least for someone who wasn't a trained killer. Like himself, for instance. What might work best was strangulation. He could wrap his hands around her neck and bear down until she stopped squirming beneath him.

A strange and unexpected thing happened as he vividly envisioned this in his head. His cock began to stiffen. As that happened, all moral considerations flew out of his head, vanishing like a handful of fairy dust, as if they'd never been real at all. And maybe they hadn't been.

His right hand was closing around her throat when he heard Lindsey's voice from almost directly above him. "Get off the little bitch, Grant. I've got this."

He angled his head around to peer up at Lindsey. The tranquilizer gun was aimed at his back and for a fleeting second he feared she would shoot him with one of those darts, sending him into unconsciousness within a few seconds. The darts were loaded with an illegally-acquired heavy-duty horse tranquilizer. Once that stuff started moving through his system, he'd be utterly helpless and at her mercy. Fortunately for his sake, he knew she needed him conscious and alive long enough to help her get this situation under control.

He scowled. "I'm handling her. I don't need your help."

There was movement from the direction of the minivan. They both glanced that way and saw a scrawny teenage boy in khaki shorts and a pale blue golf shirt backpedaling away from the minivan. Cradled in his arms was the crying baby. The boy looked terrified but determined.

He turned away from them and began to run.

Lindsey stepped forward a few feet and lifted the tranquilizer gun, squinting as she aimed down the barrel at the boy's retreating back. She squeezed the trigger, sending a dart hurtling into the darkness. The dart went stray of the mark. Grant knew this not because he saw it happen—it was impossible to track the dart's trajectory in the evening gloom—but rather because a few seconds later the boy was still on his feet and running. In a few more seconds, he would be out of the clearing and starting down the long private drive.

Lindsey lowered the tranquilizer gun. "Shit. I'm gonna have to go after them." She glanced at Grant. "Choke the bitch out, but try not to kill her. I don't want any of them dead just yet."

"Why not?"

Instead of answering his question, she took off running.

Grant watched her go for a moment, her swiftly moving long legs flashing in the moonlight. She would catch up to the boy. He had no doubt of that. He was a gangly kid struggling to hold on to a squalling infant while running for his life. She was a superbly-conditioned marathon runner. It wouldn't even be a fair contest, really.

Confident there was no need to worry about that part of the equation, he returned his full attention to the still-struggling girl. Struggling, but not making as many threats now. Her new tactic was crying and pleading, which had the unexpected effect of turning him on even more.

Grant thrust himself against her, making sure she felt his now fully erect cock. He had both hands locked around her throat now and began to steadily increase the pressure. He put his face against the side of her head and whispered in her ear. "Tell me something. Are you a virgin?"

The girl sputtered and wheezed, but no words emerged. His grip on her throat was too strong.

Grant laughed softly. "Never mind. I know you can't really talk right now. I'll tell you this, though. It's gonna be fun finding out the answer to that question."

More laughter.

He continued increasing the pressure on her throat.

It wasn't long before her struggles ceased entirely.

15

THE BOY TEMPORARILY DISAPPEARED FROM sight as he reached the edge of the clearing, obscured by trees as he went around that first wide bend in the road. This did not overly concern Lindsey. She was already closing the gap between them at a rapid rate. The only thing that worried her at all was the prospect of charging down the insanely dangerous stretch of road in the dark. One wrong step along the crazily twisting passage could send her tumbling to her death, but not going after the boy wasn't an option.

The kid was an obstacle standing in the way of everything she wanted, including a return to an outwardly normal life once she was clear of this rapidly unraveling nightmare situation. He was by no means the only thing in the way of a restoration of normality, but capturing him was her current top priority. The boy could not be allowed to reach the street, where he might theoretically flag down a ride from someone willing to take him to the nearest town. It was highly unlikely he'd be able to do that at night on a mountain road that was lightly traveled even in daylight hours, but even the slimmest possibility of it happening was an unacceptable risk. If things went that way, nothing else would matter. Her life as she'd known it would be over.

She reached the edge of the clearing and zagged right with the sharp curvature of the road, increasing her speed rather than slowing down for the sake of caution. This was a calculated risk. She sensed it was the opposite of what the boy would do. He was scared out of his mind and would be overly conscious of trying to protect the baby and not go running off the side of the road. The darkness was deeper here on this first curving stretch of the passage, which was shrouded by trees to either side. She was forced to rely partly on memory to take her in the right direction. She'd made the harrowing journey up the drive the one and only time today, but her sense of it was surprisingly clear in her mind.

In another couple moments, she zigged to the left as the road curved sharply again. The boy still wasn't in sight, but she could hear the baby crying. The sound was much closer than a few seconds ago. The trees to either side of the passage thinned out and soon disappeared entirely now that she was racing along the narrower part of the ridge. Without the trees obstructing the moonlight, she had a much clearer view of those vertigo-inducing steep drop-offs. The road went into a relatively straighter stretch and in another few seconds she saw the boy up ahead, no more than twenty feet away.

She dug down deep and found another gear. The soles of her shoes loudly slapped the hard ground as her speed increased significantly, sweat beading on her brow as her arms and legs pumped harder than ever. A few seconds later, the boy was less than ten feet in front of her. Her nostrils flared and the anticipatory grin of a hungry predator spread across her face. She flashed back to a few moments earlier back at the cabin, reliving the elation she'd felt upon driving the big blade deep into the stomach of the one Grant had called Pierce. She'd looked into his face in that moment of puncture. The memory of the way his eyes had widened as the pain registered sent a shiver of pleasure through her. It had finally happened, the thing she'd yearned for since tossing that girl off that nightclub rooftop back in college—her second kill. That it had come about in a completely unexpected way didn't matter. It had been every bit as glorious and intoxicating as she'd ever imagined, proof positive this was the right path for her.

And now she was about to bag kill number three. Another shiver of anticipatory pleasure rippled through her at the thought. She was even tempted to slow her pace ever slow slightly. By dragging this out a little longer, she'd get to savor her next victim's dread of what was about to happen to him that much more. She no longer feared him getting away. The mountain road beyond the private drive was too far away. Even now, he was almost within grabbing distance. He could probably feel her breath on the back of his neck.

She laughed. "I'm going to gut you like a pig, boy. Gonna open you all the way up and see what you look like on the fucking inside. What do you think about that?"

The boy squealed in terror.

Lindsey laughed again and reached out, scraping a long fingernail across the back of his neck. This elicited a loud shriek from the boy, who then started running harder and faster for a few moments before slowing down again. He was almost out of gas. She could tell by how wobbly his legs were. He looked like a drunkard awkwardly trying to make his way home after a long night of boozing. The baby wailed louder than ever as the boy began to stumble without quite losing his footing yet.

She slowed her pace, letting the boy get about ten feet out in front of her again. Then closer to fifteen. This would've struck her as too risky at the outset of the chase, but not now. The kid was barely running now, his loping stride more of a slow jog. He was winded and scared. In another few seconds, he'd be reduced to walking. Even a dumb kid like him had to know that would amount to surrender.

"If you stop right now, I won't kill you right away. I might even decide not to kill you at all if you cooperate and behave until I figure out what else to do with you."

The boy was walking now, but still had his back to her as he kept moving sluggishly forward. "You're lying," he said, sniffling with a quaver in his voice. "I can hear it in your . . . in your voice. You're toying with me."

Lindsey smiled. "You're smarter than the average cookie, kid. I'll give you that much at least. *Of course* I'm lying to you. You know what else? I've still got the knife I used to kill your father. His blood is fucking all over it. It's still warm, even. How's that for a kick?"

The boy's shoulders shook as he sobbed. He said nothing.

"I get why you're so broken up about it. I mean, the guy looked like a typical middle-aged douchebag with an MBA. Still, he was your dad. You loved him, right?"

The loudest sob yet came from the boy as he abruptly stopped in his tracks. After that, he heaved a big breath and said a single word in a quiet, thoroughly broken voice. "Yes."

Lindsey came to a stop about five feet behind him. "Okay, kid, here's the situation. You tried your damnedest and it wasn't good enough. Still, you tried. I can admire that. Doesn't change the fact you're about to get your ticket punched, but there is one thing I can do for you. One little act of mercy."

Still with his back to her, the boy sniffled again and said in that same defeated tone, "What's that?"

Lindsey smiled. "If you cooperate and do exactly as I tell you, I promise I won't hurt the baby."

The boy said nothing for a moment, then turned to face her. His tear-streaked face looked chalky pale in the moonlight. The baby squirmed and cried in his trembling arms. "You're lying again."

Lindsey summoned the most sincere-looking expression she could manage and gave her head a single emphatic shake. "I'm not.

Cross my heart and hope to die." She giggled for a second, but quickly stifled the sound. "Seriously. I'm kind of a bad person by normal standards, I guess. Like, *really* fucking bad. But even I've got no interest in murdering an infant. What's the point? It's not like it'd be able to testify against me in court. Unlike you. You've got to see the logic in that, right?"

He heaved another big breath. "I guess so."

Lindsey nodded. "Damn straight. It's settled, then. Put the baby on the ground and get ready to do what you're told."

After a final brief hesitation, the boy knelt and set the baby gently on the ground. Before getting up again, he gave the still-squalling infant a soft kiss on the forehead, whispering his love for his little brother.

Then he stood and stared evenly at Lindsey. "What now?"

The change in his demeanor fascinated her. There was little trace of the overwhelming fear gripping him earlier. What she heard now was resignation. Acceptance. Perhaps he was expecting a quick end to his suffering. Maybe that made it easier for him to face it now with some kind of dignity.

Poor little shit.

She had no interest in letting him off that easy.

The tranquilizer gun was still gripped in her right hand. She held it low, pointed to the ground. The knife was in her left hand. Having no use for it just now, she allowed the tranquilizer gun to slip from her fingers and fall to the ground. After kicking it aside, she shifted the knife to her right hand. Her dominant hand. Which felt apt, because she was about to use the blade as an instrument of especially brutal domination.

She waved the knife at him. "Come a little closer."

After hesitating briefly again, he took a tentative, shaky step in her direction. Then another. And another.

"That's good. Stop right there."

The boy stopped moving forward. He was short for a boy in his mid-teens. He had to stare up at her through his red-rimmed, puffy eyes. His expression conveyed fear mixed with some vague form of expectation.

Lindsey smiled. "Very good. You're cooperating nicely. I'm sure on some level your baby brother appreciates the sacrifice you're making for him. Now get on your knees."

The boy frowned, suddenly wary again. "But—"

Lindsey's face twisted in a snarl. "Shut the fuck up! Didn't I say to do exactly what the fuck I said!?"

The boy flinched in the face of her enraged outburst, jawline quivering badly as he mumbled a pitiful apology.

She waved the knife again. "That's right, you're fucking sorry. You're about the sorriest little shit on the planet, matter of fact. No more fucking around, kid. I get anything less than instant, total obedience from you this time, I may have to break that promise I made about not hurting your brother."

The kid started blubbering again when she said this. "Don't. Please . . . please don't."

Lindsey's thin smile was pitiless. "On your knees. *Now.*"

The boy dropped to his knees.

Lindsey let out a slow exhalation of breath and allowed herself a moment to luxuriate in the anticipation of what she was about to do. While those moments of intense euphoria she'd experienced when murdering this boy's father had been amazing, it'd happened so suddenly and was over almost as soon as it began. This was different. The situation back at the cabin was contained, under control. There were no other complications here to deal with. She could do whatever she wanted at this point. There was no one around to see what she was doing or intervene.

She approached the kneeling boy and held the blade up to his face. "See that? That's your father's blood, like I said. I want you to lick up as much of that blood as you can."

She turned the knife, holding it so a side of the blade was almost pressed to his lips. Fat tears started spilling from the boy's eyes again. He sniffled and whined. Behind him, the baby cried and squirmed around on the ground.

"Do it, you pathetic piece of shit. You already know the price of disobedience. You've got about five seconds to start licking before I punt that brother of yours into the fucking valley."

Still sniffling, the boy stuck out his tongue and tentatively began licking at the coagulating blood coating the blade. Lindsey shivered in sudden arousal. This was the first time she'd ever gotten to do this kind of thing to someone she actually intended to kill. It was sort of similar to some of the more aggressive BDSM scenarios she acted out with Grant in their basement dungeon, but doing it for real with an actual victim got her juices flowing like nothing else ever had before. She still figured she'd be done with Grant one way or another after this was over, but maybe they could have one last good hard fuck later tonight. Maybe she'd even kill him at his moment of orgasm.

Wouldn't that be a kick?

Apparently sensing her drifting attention, the boy surprised her by making a grab for the knife. She yelped and ripped it away from him when he tried twisting it out of her hand. The blade sliced deep across his fingers, cutting nearly to the bone. In the next instant, he surged to his feet and made a second grab for the knife while she was still somewhat startled. She spun away and his bleeding fingers missed grabbing onto her wrist by a small fraction of an inch. He tackled her from behind and they spent some moments rolling around on the ground and thrashing at each other. The boy was scrawny, but his strength surprised her. At one point he managed to land a punch to her jaw that made her teeth clamp together. She squealed in pain as she bit her tongue and felt blood in her mouth. In that moment, she felt afraid for the first time since her bathroom struggle with Grant.

Fuck this.

She jerked her head to the side in time to avoid another bone-crunching punch to the jaw and lashed out blindly with the knife, driving the tip of the blade into one of the boy's eyes. He screamed in shrill agony and rolled quickly away from her.

Breathing heavily, she summoned all her strength and sat up. Then she got to her feet and spun about until she saw the boy. He was on his knees about six feet away, facing away from her. He had his hands to his face and was screaming ceaselessly. Apparently it hurt like hell to have steel slammed into your eyeball. Lindsey's fear drained away in an instant. The boy had taken a shot and lost. She couldn't blame him. It was what anyone who wasn't a total pussy would do. He'd probably even been playing along to a certain extent, hoping for just the kind of opportunity he'd gotten. Fair play, but it was over now, and her interest in dragging this out was gone.

She walked up to him and kicked him hard in the small of the back. He yelped and pitched forward, landing face-down in the dirt. She dropped to her knees beside him, raised the knife high over her head, and brought it down fast, slamming it into his back up to the hilt. He screamed and screamed again when she ripped the blade out. He braced his hands on the ground and shakily tried to push himself up.

She smiled. "You're not going anywhere, fucker."

The big blade punched into his back again and this time she kept it there a minute, twisting it as she listened to him unleash several of the loudest screams she'd ever heard. When she finally took it out again, she rolled him over and dragged the blade across his throat. This was a much deeper throat wound than the one she'd inflicted on the boy's father. A great gout of blood leaped out of the hole in his flesh, adding to the drenching she'd already taken. She sat there next to the boy a while longer, watching the blood flow slow to a gurgle and then stop altogether.

She sighed. "You were a tough one, kid. I'll give you that. *Fuck.*"

Getting to her feet again, she took hold of the dead boy's wrists and dragged him over to a side of the ridge. Then she pushed at him with her foot and sent him rolling down into the darkness of the valley below. She stood there a moment and listened to his body roll and crash against outcroppings of rock and tree stumps.

When the tumbling corpse ceased making any discernible noise, she walked over to the baby and stared down at it. The infant stared up at her with tiny eyes that looked glassy in the moonlight. Eyes devoid of true comprehension. There was no way it could grasp what had happened here. That part of what she'd told the teenager hadn't been a lie. She had no interest in murdering the little one. Not because she had any kind of hangup about going one step too far. Instead, she simply couldn't be bothered. She didn't want to carry it up to the cabin and have to listen to its squalling all night. In truth, she didn't have to do a damned thing. She could just leave it right here. Sooner or later, nature would take its course. The road was too distant to worry about it crawling out that way. It would either die on the spot or an animal would snag it and carry it away. She was fine with either outcome.

After retrieving the tranquilizer gun, she gave the crying baby one last glance, then started the journey back up to the cabin. She'd gone about fifty feet in that direction when a dirty, scraggly-haired hermit in his tattered rags came scrambling up over the side of the ridge and onto the road.

The hermit took a cautious look around with his darting, crazy-looking eyes.

Then he snatched up the baby and went back over the side.

16

THE MAN AND WOMAN WHO'D abducted Jorge barely took note of him as they came racing down the stairs. The woman did cast one quick glance in his direction as they went rushing by, but she appeared unconcerned he'd managed to make the chair topple over. This was unsurprising. His hope of snapping a leg of the chair by causing it to fall backward at an angle had gone unfulfilled. The chair remained intact and his bindings as secure as ever. As far as he could tell, they hadn't loosened at all in the fall.

Also, in that moment, they had bigger things to worry about. More people had arrived at the cabin. That they hadn't been expecting these new arrivals was apparent in their panicked demeanors. A middle-aged, white-haired man opened the front door and stepped into the cabin before they could block his entrance. Within seconds, it was clear the white-haired man was related to his abductors. It was also clear he was shocked by what he discovered upon entering the cabin. Jorge saw right away the man was, unlike his younger relations, possessed of some level of actual integrity. He was the kind of man who would have no interest in being a party to things like torture and murder.

For a few fleeting moments, Jorge had allowed his hopes to soar, believing this man represented his best chance of deliverance from this horrendous situation. He'd even attempted to alert the man to the deadly nature of the circumstances he'd stepped into by shouting indignantly every time the one named Grant lied about the situation, which was virtually every time he opened his mouth.

Hope soon gave way to despair, however, when the female abductor rushed at the older man with a big-ass knife and started ripping his stomach open. From his position on the floor, Jorge had shuddered in revulsion. He'd never seen anyone killed right in front of him like that. It was beyond unsettling. He felt bile rise into his throat multiple times. This triggered a new fear. The woman's panties were still lodged in his throat, the strips of duct tape still in place over his mouth. He couldn't allow himself to vomit, regardless of how sickened he was by the bloody events he was witnessing. He didn't want to go out like that, choking on his own puke like some hopeless heroin addict. Hell, he didn't want to go out at all, but especially not like that, completely helpless to do anything about it.

Then Jorge heard other voices even as the white-haired man's body collapsed to the floor. A young girl's voice, most prominently. The man's family had made the journey up to the cabin with him. Jorge had mixed feelings about that. The idea of children out there was horrifying, because the demented couple who'd taken him had already shown there were no lengths to which they would not go to contain the situation. That would definitely include murdering an entire family of people related to them, if necessary.

On the other hand, more people out there meant a greater chance of at least one of them getting away and alerting the cops. One of them might even be able to get on a phone and call 911, providing they were able to react quickly enough.

All hell broke loose as the couple rushed outside and started grappling with the rest of the dead man's family. Jorge heard shouts, screams, and other sounds of struggle. There were definitely multiple other people out there. And, judging from the cries he heard, one baby. His soul experienced despair again when he heard those cries.

He started yanking at his bonds again as he listened to the horrific sounds of struggle from outside, working himself into a frenzy but accomplishing little as the chair rocked around a bit on the floor. Despite his lack of progress, he didn't allow himself to stop or give up. If the couple managed to subdue or kill the dead man's other family members, they would be back in here to deal with him before long. He had to try to get loose while he had the opportunity, even if his chances of success seemed remote verging on impossible.

As he struggled, he again thought about what his father called the Mendez family curse, that awful string of bad luck incidents stretching back over decades and generations. Unlike his father, he'd never been a slave to superstition. He didn't believe in curses or black magic or any of that kind of nonsense. By allowing himself to perish here, some of his living relations would see what had befallen him as the strongest possible proof the curse was real. Not wanting that to happen drove him nearly as much as his basic desire to keep on living.

He kept at it even as the sounds of struggle outside died down. There were no more shouts or screams, just some animalistic grunting that struck him as vaguely sexual. Not even wanting to think about what that implied, he redoubled his efforts yet again and, for the first time, felt the tiniest increment of give around his left ankle. His heart started racing as he twisted his foot and heard the wood creak. That leg of the chair was ever so slightly damaged.

Then he heard footsteps on the porch and felt despair yet again. All that effort had finally started paying off in a very small way. It was something, though. A start. What he'd been hoping so desperately for all along. He hadn't gotten it done quite fast enough.

There was another sound from the porch. Heavy thumps. Someone was dragging something into the cabin. Jorge craned his head around in time to see Grant dragging a dead or unconscious teenage girl inside. Her arms were limp and her head lolled around as he pulled her across the floor.

After dumping the girl somewhere on the other side of the table, Grant started back toward the door, but stopped and glanced over at Jorge, who was still trying to twist his ankle against the weakened leg of the chair. "Stop doing that," he said, frowning. "I mean it, hombre. Hear me?"

Jorge stopped twisting his ankle and sighed.

He nodded.

Grant pointed a finger at him. "I'm serious. You don't want to die yet, do you?"

Jorge shook his head.

"Good." His abductor grinned. "Stay right there."

He laughed as he walked back out the door, sounding in surprisingly good spirits for a man embroiled in a situation spiraling out of control.

A few seconds later, Jorge heard more thumps from the porch. This time Grant dragged in an unconscious grown woman. A feathered tranquilizer dart protruded from her neck. She was older than the girl by maybe twenty years. The distinct familial resemblance told Jorge she was likely the girl's mother.

There was no sign yet of Lindsey, nor had he heard Grant talking with her these last couple times he'd gone in and out of the cabin. Perhaps she was chasing down yet another family member. Come to think of it, it'd been a while since he'd last heard the baby's cries. Her absence might have something to do with that. Thinking about what that might imply brought another of those trickles of nausea to the back of his throat.

Grant deposited the mother on the floor alongside her daughter.

He moved back a few steps and stared at them a moment, frowning as he scratched the back of his head. Jorge's view of the woman and girl was impeded slightly by the table and other chairs, but he did see the fingers of the daughter's outstretched right hand twitch one time.

Still alive, then.

For now.

Grant took a roll of duct tape from the table and went to work wrapping it around the wrists and ankles of his female captives. He worked fast, clearly interested in securing them only in a basic way before they could regain consciousness. Perhaps when Lindsey returned—if she did—they would work together at getting them into chairs and bound in a more elaborate way.

But what if Lindsey *wasn't* coming back? Maybe she'd died in the struggle out there. It didn't seem likely, but it was possible. Never in his life had Jorge actively wished for the death of another person. His mind flashed back to the moment when that evil woman aimed the tranquilizer gun at him and pulled the trigger. That smugly superior look on her face. She and her husband were obviously both dangerous, but if he had his pick of one to eliminate from the equation, he'd pick her in a heartbeat. He sensed she was the catalyst behind all of this. The most cunning and calculating of the two by a mile. Against only Grant, he might yet stand a chance of surviving. It'd still be a bleakly slim chance, but it'd be better than nothing.

Grant dropped the depleted roll of duct tape on the table and retrieved something else from its surface. A moment later, he was kneeling next to the teenager. Then came some kind of cutting sound. It took Jorge a moment to recognize it as the tearing of fabric. He struggled to crane his head around still farther. Doing this caused a painful crick in his neck, but he was soon able to see that Grant was sinking to yet another level of depravity. It shouldn't have surprised him. These people were clearly capable of anything. Yet he still felt intensely disgusted when he saw Grant cutting away the younger girl's clothes and tossing aside the shredded pieces of fabric. Getting it all removed required a fair amount of work, including lifting her up and turning her side to side multiple times. Soon he had her down to her underwear.

She began to stir slightly as Grant cut away her bra. Her eyes remained shut as he flicked the bra away and, in an oddly tentative way, lowered a hand to one of her breasts and began to gently squeeze it. He groaned in arousal and squeezed her other breast, harder this time.

Then Jorge heard footsteps on the porch outside.

Lindsey came back into the cabin.

Jorge felt like crying when he turned his head and saw her. Her return signaled a massive blow to the faint and dying hopes of survival to which he'd still been clinging. Not only that, but she had a lot more blood on her now. Her arms, face, and shirt were drenched in red. Someone else had died out there at her hands tonight. Some other member of this poor family. Maybe the baby, but not just the baby. Someone else, some brave young soul, had tried to carry the infant away from this nightmare. Had tried to be a hero.

Someone who wound up dead instead.

Jorge's eyes brimmed with tears.

It was over. All hope was lost. There was only dying left to do, along with a whole lot of suffering and misery.

17

GRANT GASPED AND JERKED HIS hand away from the girl's chest when he heard his wife come into the cabin. He shot to his feet and moved away from the girl, who was mumbling again and stirring closer to consciousness. His face flushed red from embarrassment at having been caught in the act of molesting the helpless girl. He felt more like an awkward and naughty schoolboy than a grown man when he met Lindsey's withering gaze.

She stood there staring at him from the open doorway a moment before turning away from him to close and lock the door. "What the actual fuck were you doing with that girl?" she asked, after turning to face him again. "Were you about to rape her?"

Grant scowled. "No. Of course not."

Even to his own ears, he sounded defensive and cagey.

Stepping over the body of the man she'd murdered earlier, Lindsey walked over to where he'd dumped the bound women and sat on her haunches as she gave them a once-over. She frowned as she tested and pulled at the layers of duct tape wound around the teenager's ankles.

Turning her head about, she looked first at Grant, then at the cluttered surface of the table, nodding as she did so. "I need more of that tape. The way you did this would never hold. They could easily chew the tape off their wrists given the chance."

Grant's face reddened again, this time more from a burgeoning anger than from embarrassment. He'd never cared for being chastised by anyone for anything, but criticism of any kind was especially galling coming from the woman who'd betrayed him by fucking his cousin. The rage that had gripped him while attempting to strangle her earlier was flickering to life again.

Lindsey looked at him and rolled her eyes in disdain when she saw how angry he was getting. "Fuck it. I'll get it myself, you sensitive little baby."

She got to her feet, grabbed the tape roll he'd used earlier as well as an extra one, and resumed squatting alongside their new captives. Over the next several minutes, she worked at reinforcing the work Grant had already done, interweaving numerous layers of tape between wrists and ankles. She also sealed their mouths shut. By the time she was satisfied with what she'd done, she'd used up all the tape on both rolls.

Standing up again, she directed a smirk at Grant. "They won't be chewing their way loose from that any time soon."

He nodded. "Okay."

He could see she was right. Given the amount of tape she'd used, the only hope the mother and daughter had of walking out of here would be for someone to cut them free of their bonds. Unless someone else unexpected showed up, the odds of that happening were close to nil.

Lindsey's smirk deepened. "Come on, baby. Tell the truth. You *were* thinking of violating that poor, innocent little girl, weren't you?" She laughed when she saw his eyes widen with anger again. "No need to get bent out of shape about it. We both know what I saw.

I'm not judging you for it."

His brow furrowed when she said this, confusion beginning to drive back some of the anger. "You're not? Really?"

She shook her head. "Of course not. How could I? Baby, take a look around you." She turned in a slow semi-circle, gesturing with her hand in a way meant to encompass all the plentiful evidence of violence and depravity in the cabin, which currently looked a bit like it'd been used by fugitive members of the Manson family during a long weekend of drug-fueled murderous shenanigans. "We're way past moral considerations of any kind here. There's no bottom to this anymore, no lower place we can go. Even the devil would be disgusted with us. You know what that means?"

Grant had an inkling, but he still couldn't quite come out and say it. Not until she said it first. He frowned again. "What does it mean?"

She smiled. "It means there are no boundaries. No restrictions. It means you can indulge in all the sickest desires you've ever harbored. You want to fuck that girl? Go ahead. I won't stop you. Hell, I'll even help hold her down."

Grant almost couldn't believe what he was hearing. In his heart, he knew the truth at the heart of what she was saying. There was no coming back from the things they'd done tonight. Cleaning up the physical mess and burning the evidence would never scrub their tainted souls clean. Yet a small part of him was still clinging to a lifetime of societal conditioning. He was astonished by the depths to which they'd sunk within such a short time. What had been intended as a relatively small act of dark marital bonding had exploded into something far beyond that. Even now, it was hard to truly comprehend the scope of it all.

"Did you kill the other kid? That boy?"

She nodded.

"And the baby?"

Her mischievous smile made her look extra cute even beneath

the coating of gore on her face. "Gone, too."

From the floor came an anguished cry. The daughter was fully awake now and glaring at them. Her mother was beginning to stir slightly, but her eyes were still closed. The girl hurled angry curses at them that were almost fully intelligible despite the layers of duct tape covering her mouth. Tears welled in her eyes and spilled down the sides of her head. The display of emotion over additional losses tugged very faintly at something inside Grant, but the feeling evaporated almost instantly. He recognized it now as nothing other than a helpless mental reflex, an echo of something that had died within him rather than a real spark of humanity.

Lindsey looked at Grant, her expression shifting as her features took on a more seductive cast. "I'll help you with her now if you want, but to tell you the truth, I'd rather you use that hard fucking dick on me."

Without another word, she pulled the formerly white, blood-spattered shirt off over head and let it drop to the floor. She looked him in the eye as she unhooked her bra and cast it aside, too. After stepping out of her shoes, she wriggled out of her denim shorts and panties and stood wantonly naked before him. His cock strained painfully against the fabric of his jeans as he stared at her gorgeous naked body. He was still experiencing some residual emotional distress in the wake of seeing those enraging photos, but as far as Grant was concerned, everything about her on a physical level remained perfect. Her body was exquisitely toned from all the running she did. Unlike a lot of women who worked hard to stay fit, however, her frame was not overly muscular, retaining a lush feminine softness. Her breasts were a nice size. Bigger than average, but not too big. The curvature of her figure was also incredibly pleasing.

Compared to the naked girl on the floor, his wife was an objectively superior physical specimen. Lindsey was a grown woman, whereas his young captive was still developing. Under ordinary circumstances, choosing Lindsey would be a given. His lust for her continued to intensify the longer he stared at her enticing naked form, but he kept thinking about the many intriguing things she'd said. She'd essentially issued him a free pass to do as he wished with the girl without fear of marital consequences. In a way, following through on that almost felt sort of necessary. Perhaps by doing so, it might balance the scales somewhat, make things even between them again. Maybe they'd even be able to go forward as a couple after tonight, something he wouldn't have believed possible just a short while ago.

He looked at the girl and imagined savagely fucking her while she cried for her lost family members. As a newly uninhibited wallower in filth and evil, the idea was deeply appealing on an animal level. He could almost see himself laughing in her face as he repeatedly thrust into her hard enough to hurt.

Lindsey came over to him and grabbed him by the crotch of his jeans, squeezing hard. He groaned as his cock spasmed and was just able to hold himself back from the brink of early ejaculation. She squeezed hard again, twisting this time. He whined and came even closer to creaming his jeans.

Lindsey laughed. "Let that be a lesson to you. There's no one like me. Not for you. Ever. Get out of your fucking clothes, you piece of shit."

Grant needed no further inducement. It was like they were in his basement dungeon back home with Lindsey in her usual role of dominating mistress, except she wasn't wearing the usual black latex and had no whip to crack at him.

He began tearing his clothes off as fast as he could manage. While he was undressing, she pulled a chair away from the table and turned it so it was facing the bound women. At her direction, he sat in the chair, his inflamed cock standing up like a flagpole. He spread his legs wide as she put her back to him and lowered herself to his crotch in the reverse cowgirl position. Gasping loudly at the moment of penetration, he grabbed her by the waist for something to hold onto, otherwise he would've come immediately. She shoved his hands away and began bouncing atop him with abandon. Within seconds, she was screaming and warning him not to come too soon.

By then, however, he already knew there was no way he'd be able to last longer than maybe another minute. The buildup to this had been too intense. Knowing for certain that moment of orgasm wasn't far away, he leaned to his left in order to see around his wife and get a clear view of the girl's face. The moment he saw that teary visage, his dick became even stiffer. He stared at the girl through the rest of it, imagining it was her lithe little body atop him rather than that of his wife. He whined at the intensity of the pleasure coursing through his body in those moments.

An instant later, he exploded inside Lindsey.

She screamed.

There was intense ecstasy in that sound, but there was also rage. Even as the waves of euphoria continued washing through him, she climbed off his still-inflamed cock and reached around him to grab something from the table. Before he could ask her what she was doing, she dropped to her knees on the floor, raised the long nail high above her head, and slammed it down.

Along with several other items, they had acquired the oversized nails during a recent shopping expedition to a hardware store. The purchases they made that day were all in preparation for the murder they intended to commit during their honeymoon trip across the country. That had been a fun day. After noticing that they'd been browsing for an extended time, a store employee offered his assistance. Based on the quantity and variety of items in their shopping cart, he assumed they were prepping for a big home improvement project.

They teased the employee with implications of darker reasons behind some of the things they were buying. Mostly it was Lindsey doing this, of course. She was always the bolder one. This one with a propensity for risky behavior, but Grant hadn't been overly worried at the time. The plan was to commit murder on the other side of the country. A one-time, isolated event. This guy would never hear about it and authorities would have no reason to ever question him. The employee played along, undoubtedly never believing for a second that this prosperous and attractive young couple would ever actually do anything truly terrible. The big nails were his suggestion.

"For all your crucifixion needs," had been his witty remark at the time.

Grant and Lindsey smiled and laughed. They eyed the nails and exchanged playful glances. The five-inch nails were significantly thicker than any nails either had ever used for common household purposes. Lindsey jokingly called them "railroad spikes". This was an extreme exaggeration, but they both instantly saw the potential the nails had as useful torture accessories.

And now, for the first time, one of them was being put to use.

The tip of the nail punched through duct tape and the flesh beneath it, sliding deep into the girl's mouth and leaving perhaps slightly more than an inch of shiny steel protruding from her cheek.

Awake now, the girl's mother started screaming.

18

THE GIRL'S EYES BUGGED OPEN wide as the pain caused her to sit bolt upright. Lindsey punched her in the face, driving the nail in slightly deeper even as the head of the nail painfully scraped the backs of her fingers. She laughed as the girl flopped back down to the floor and squealed in agony.

The mother was making loud sounds of distress while attempting to scoot closer to her daughter. It was sort of a useless gesture. There was nothing practical she could do to help with her hands wrapped in so much tape, but the motherly instinct to protect compelled her to try anyway.

Lindsey got to her feet and kicked the woman in the face. There was a loud crunch of cartilage as her nose snapped and blood gushed down over her tape-covered chin. She screamed again as she flopped onto her back and stared up at the ceiling through eyes overflowing with tears.

The visages of both women were a study in abject misery. Lindsey found this a pleasing sight to behold. They looked so helpless and hopeless. Imagining the psychological torment they must be in also pleased her. Most gratifying of all, however, was knowing they were completely under her control. It was a glorious feeling, having that kind of power over other human beings.

She turned away from them and faced her husband with a sneer. "I told you not to come too fast, you fucking asshole, but you didn't listen. You were thinking of that little cunt when it happened, weren't you? Well, look at the bitch now. She's got a fucking nail in her face. Still wanna fuck her?"

Grant withered under the intensity of her glare, averting his gaze as he spoke in a voice barely above a whisper. "I'm sorry."

He sounded strangely subdued, perhaps even shocked by the sudden savagery of what she'd done. He might even be temporarily in the grip of one of his occasional fake moral quandaries. She could imagine the thoughts rolling around in his stupid head.

How did I allow myself to sink to this level? Why did you let this happen, God? Why, why, why?

She snorted.

He was an idiot. A fucking diletantte. He'd gone along with the whole murder scheme largely to please her. She was the one with the real passion for this stuff. If she hadn't come along, he likely would've been content to spend the rest of his life keeping his darker urges contained to the realm of fantasy. At heart, he was a dithering coward. She could only feel contempt for someone like that. The only positive was that she'd learned the truth about him relatively early on.

"Sorry's not good enough." She sighed and shook her head. "Fuck it. I'm gonna go take a shower and get all this blood off me."

He looked at her now, a corner of his mouth lifting in a small smirk. "What's the point? You'll only get more on you later."

She showed him a smirk of her own. "Okay, you want to know the truth? That one-minute fuck did not satisfy me. Not even close.

So, since you have failed utterly in your husbandly duties, *again*, I'm gonna take a few minutes to take care of my own damn self. And, hey, you know what else would be swell? It'd be really super-awesome if you'd try your hardest not to fuck anything else up while I'm gone."

He frowned. "Me? None of this mess is my fault. If we'd stuck to the plan—"

Surprising even herself, she backhanded him across the face, making him yelp in pain as a thin trickle of blood began to leak from a nostril. Despite the rage frothing inside her, she experienced a small flicker of regret almost immediately. Yes, she was angry with him, *extremely* angry, but she needed to remember how close he'd come to killing her while in a rage of his own. She sensed she hadn't quite pushed him over the edge again yet, but it might happen if she continued lashing out at him so severely.

He rubbed his chin and gave her a stern look. "I guess I get why you're upset, but you don't want to do that again. I mean it. You hear me?"

She seethed inside at this warning, but managed to suppress her instinct to retort with something equally provocative. Despite everything, the evening remained rife with potential. She had multiple captive human beings at her mercy and was yearning to exercise her sadistic imagination on all of them. Going to war with Grant again might ruin all of that.

She huffed out a begrudging sigh. "Fine. Possibly I overreacted. But I'm still taking that shower. Please don't kill any of them while I'm gone."

He glared at her a moment longer before his expression softened. "Oh, don't worry," he said, smiling. "I won't start the fun without you. I'm not the one who perforated a girl's face in a moment of sexual frustration, after all. I've got more restraint than that."

Lindsey again held back the instinct to lash out.

Fine. Let him have the last word. For now. The son of a bitch may yet get what's coming to him.

She rolled her eyes to express her disdain, but kept her mouth shut as she moved away from him and climbed the stairs to the loft.

19

HE'D HAD A NAME ONCE, back in the days when he lived and worked among men, but those days had ended long ago. Now, after decades of living alone in the woods, he no longer recalled what that name had been. In truth, he rarely attempted to remember anything from that previous existence. On the rare occasion when some faint memory of that time floated close to the surface of his conscious mind, he immediately shoved it back into the darkest recesses of his psyche. That was where the past belonged. Buried. Locked down in the shadows. Memories of those painful years couldn't hurt him there.

The old hermit lived in a decrepit shack deep in the woods. He'd built it from scavenged materials gathered from various construction sites scattered across the mountainous region, mostly discarded wood scraps no one would ever miss. The cabin had no windows. His construction skills were too primitive for that, his access to the necessary materials too limited. He had a few rusted pots and pans. Some utensils for eating. Tools for hunting. There was no electricity. He kept warm in the winter by swaddling himself in tattered blankets stolen from the privately-owned cabins he sometimes broke into when his need for critical supplies became too great. This was something he did only when absolutely necessary. Too much of that kind of thing might attract a level of attention he didn't want. He didn't want to be forced out of hiding or arrested. He'd rather die than return to the world of men.

With the weather beginning to turn cold again, however, a need to replace the tattered old blankets he'd stolen years ago had arisen. Last night had been miserable, with temperatures dropping to a level far lower than usual for this time of year. Not wishing to endure another night like that, he'd ventured out to the nearest cabin in the area, one he knew was often unoccupied for many weeks at a time. A private drive to the cabin had been carved from the top of a steep mountain ridge. For the old hermit, scaling the ridge in order to walk up to the cabin would not present a huge obstacle. He'd become a highly skilled climber during his decades in the woods.

Climbing up the side of the ridge would, of course, be more difficult at night than in the daytime, but he wasn't overly concerned about that. He would have to go a bit slower and be more careful than usual. What he hadn't counted on was the bloody tableau that greeted him at the top of the ridge. He'd heard the screaming and sounds of struggle even before reaching the top and had considered retreat. Though he remained remarkably agile for someone his age, he was an old man. Also, he currently had nothing he could use as a weapon on his person. Without the means to defend himself, putting himself in the middle of a violent situation was not something he was particularly keen to do.

The sounds he was hearing were not the kind that would originate from an ordinary fight. The people engaged in the struggle at the top of the ridge were trying desperately to kill each other. He'd heard similar sounds before. Hearing them now triggered unwanted memories of things he never wanted to think about again. Memories of blood and thunder, screams and pain. His many scars throbbed and his head filled with hateful images as a part of him that had remained dormant for many years threatened to awaken.

In the end, sheer curiosity compelled him to take a look at what was happening. He peeked over the edge of the ridge and watched as a beautiful young woman fought viciously with an even younger boy, who looked to be somewhere in his mid-teens. There was a squalling infant on the ground nearby, too. The woman eventually wound up getting the upper hand. She then appeared to take great delight in murdering the boy, drawing it out and making it as agonizing as possible. The old hermit hadn't seen anything like it in a long time. Seeing it now made his scars throb uncomfortably again.

After the boy was dead, the woman tossed his corpse over the other side of the ridge. The hermit experienced a tense moment when she first took hold of the boy's limp wrists, fearing she would drag the body this way and spy him peeping out at her. Fortunately, that didn't happen.

She then spent some moments staring at the crying baby, apparently weighing what to do about it. He thought she might kill it or take it with her, anything but what she actually did. Shortly after she turned away from it and began the walk back up to the cabin, an impulse caused him to scramble the rest of the way up the ridge and grab the baby.

The journey back down the side of the ridge was far more harrowing than it ever had been before. With the baby held tightly in the crook of one arm, he had to be exceedingly careful with each step down. It took quite a bit longer than it normally would, but he eventually made it down safely.

And now here he was back in his shack, with the baby resting atop the rickety wooden crate where he took his meals most nights. He sat on another crate in the dim lantern light and stared at the infant as it squealed and flailed helplessly with its little pink fists.

He'd had a son once.

David. That had been his name.

The hermit's hands curled into fists as he gritted his teeth and his head filled with echoes of fearsome thunder. Outside the shack, it was quiet.

Inside, a storm was raging.

20

THE NAKED GIRL ON THE floor was still breathing. Grant could tell that much from the miserable mewling sounds she was making. She was also gagging on the nail wedged deep in her mouth and the blood filling her throat. He worried she'd soon choke to death if he didn't remove the nail and duct tape from her mouth and turn her onto her side. This had nothing to do with any concern for her well-being. They were far past that. The girl and her mother were both already doomed. Too much had happened. It was like Lindsey had said, there was no coming back from this. He was pissed at her and hated to give her any level of credit for anything, but she was undeniably right about that.

So, yes, the girl was doomed no matter what, but he didn't want her to perish just yet. He was no longer in the fevered state of erotic obsession he'd been in prior to fucking Lindsey, but he still found the girl's nude body compellling. She had a belly button piercing, a little silver heart right in the middle of her navel. The only tattoo she had was a small shamrock on her right shoulder. It was so bright green he figured she'd gotten it recently, probably within the last few months. He wondered if she'd had to get parental permission for these minor body modifications. Probably, he guessed, though he wasn't entirely sure where the law stood on such things. For all he knew, she'd turned eighteen recently and was legally able to make such decisions for herself. He made a mental note to check the minivan later. She might have a purse out there with her ID in it.

He decided he *would* remove the nail and do whatever else necessary to stave off her demise a bit longer. Despite this, he did not immediately act to help her. A sudden onset of melancholy kept him in the chair as his mind began to travel along dark corridors. In those moments, he realized it didn't matter how hard they worked to cover up what had happened here. They could try to erase physical evidence by burning the place to the ground, but he had little doubt the police would suspect them anyway. He'd seen too many crime documentaries in which people tried to cover up their dirty deeds in a similar way while concocting a preposterous cover story. No matter how careful or detail-oriented the perpetrators were, the cops were usually pretty adept at sniffing out the truth. An investigation would reveal his and Lindsey's shared deep fascination with true crime stories and from there it wouldn't take much to start connecting the dots. On top of all that, a fire might not even destroy all the physical evidence. Most of it, maybe, but damning traces would probably remain.

There was only one viable way out and it was a longshot. They would have to act fast, before the crime scene was discovered. Instead of attempting to cover up the crime by setting the cabin ablaze, they would get together as much money as they could and escape to some country with no extradition treaty. That might not keep them free forever, but it might give them time to establish new identities and escape to yet another location. If they worked it just right, they might yet manage to get away with everything.

He stewed over this conclusion a moment longer before heaving a sigh. The plan struck him as fundamentally sound with the exception of one major flaw. It was based on the assumption he and Lindsey would stay together after leaving this place. He thought of all the things that had happened between them tonight and, with a slightly heavy heart, realized a continued partnership with her would in all likelihood be untenable. There was too much animosity, too much water under the bridge, and setting it right would be next to impossible.

Aside from all that, he might have a better chance of eluding capture as a man traveling alone. After all, the authorities would at least initially be hunting a couple. Before leaving the country, he would have to kill Lindsey and dump her body in some other remote location, a place where it hopefully wouldn't be discovered for a long time.

Grant was under no illusions. He was certain Lindsey was thinking similar things up there in the shower. His wife was a genuinely hardcore bitch. Ruthless and merciless in ways that gave even him pause. That thing with the baby. Jesus. In her place, he didn't know if he could've done it. He would have to remain vigilant and wary of her until he decided the time was right to kill her.

And yet . . . his melancholy wasn't only about Lindsey and how difficult it would be to get away after doing something like this. He was able to think more clearly post-orgasm, which meant certain realities of the situation were weighing on him more heavily now.

These women on the floor were a far cry from the type of anonymous victim he'd envisioned. He didn't know them extremely well, but he knew them. They were his relatives. The girl's blood carried his DNA. There was something obscene about having to kill her, especially, even if there was no way around it. Even worse was the prospect of closer relatives, parents or siblings, hearing about what they'd done. They would be devastated. Inconsolable. For a moment, he found this aspect of it almost overwhelming. His mother would, of course, be in deep denial at first, but at some point accepting the truth of it all would be unavoidable. He imagined the overwhelming horror she would feel when it truly hit her. In the next few moments, melancholia was replaced by something close to despair. A part of him suddenly, desperately wished he could take it all back and go back to leading a proper, normal life. He made a sound somewhere between a laugh and a sob at how absurdly impossible that was now.

He was snapped out of his sad funk by the girl's gagging sounds abruptly getting much louder. Sliding out of the chair, he dropped to his knees next to her, braced one hand against her chest to hold her still, and began the process of extracting the big nail. She gagged harder than ever and stared up at him through watery eyes as he continued pulling at the nail. He saw pleading in those eyes. A level of desperation almost beyond comprehension.

After he was finished pulling out the nail, he set it on the floor and ripped the duct tape off the girl's face. A choked half-scream escaped her lips as Grant turned her onto her side and began encouraging her to hack out the blood. She spat out several large globs of the red stuff mixed with phlegm. After that, she continued coughing and spitting, but the bits of spittle that emerged mostly came out clear. Satisfied she'd successfully cleared her throat of obstruction, he gently eased her onto her back.

Grant smiled. "There you go. All better now?"

Her eyes filled with fresh tears as she sniffled and said, "Please don't kill me. I'm pregnant."

Grant's smile slipped as his mouth opened and he gaped at her in stunned confusion for a moment. Then he gave his head a hard shake and said, "Wait . . . what?"

She loudly cleared her throat and swallowed with obvious difficulty. Then, in a much clearer and steadier voice, she repeated what she'd already said: "I'm pregnant. Six weeks fucking pregnant. I found out yesterday."

Grant grunted and shook his head again. "Holy shit."

21

PIPER WEATHERBY WAS NOT A stupid woman. She knew she was caught up in a desperate and possibly hopeless situation. Her chances of surviving the night were close to nonexistent. Unfortunately, the same was true for Kelsey, who was now claiming to be pregnant. The declaration came as an immense shock to her mother, who hadn't even known the girl was seeing any boy on a serious basis.

Not that anything resembling a serious relationship was a prerequisite for getting pregnant. At no point in her life had she ever been that naive. Even if she had been, the arrival of her third child so long after the births of Rory and Kelsey would've disabused her of the notion. Baby Vance was the result of one of her numerous brief hookups with other men. She couldn't even be one-hundred percent certain who the real father was, but she knew for an absolute fact it wasn't Pierce.

All this time later, she was still sometimes baffled by her decision to go forward with the pregnancy. Even in this era of backwards lawmakers relentlessly tightening the laws regarding abortion access, terminating the pregnancy would've been by far the easier way to go. For one thing, it would've led to far fewer life complications. She'd enjoyed the greater freedom that had been hers with Rory and Kelsey getting old enough to look after themselves for the most part. By opting to keep the baby, she was also choosing to reduce that level of freedom by a significant degree. In the end, however, she simply hadn't been able to go through with ending the life growing inside her.

The one way in which she'd been fortunate was Pierce's perpetual obliviousness. Despite their drastically reduced frequency of intercourse in recent years—they rarely fucked more than once every month or two—he never once doubted he was the father. Of course not. His ego wouldn't have allowed for the possibility back then. He was a man's man. King of his castle. Lord of all he surveyed. No one would dare intrude on his territory. All that standard alpha-male bullshit. Though it was a bit of a stretch, the timing had been such that she could get away with passing the pregnancy off as the product of one of their rare couplings.

It helped that he'd still been wrapped up in his work back then. If she'd gotten knocked up after his recent retirement, she almost certainly would've gone the termination route. In retirement, with so much less to occupy his mind and time, he'd become much more inquisitive about where she went every day and how she spent her time. Though he hadn't come out and accused her of cheating on him, she knew he'd become suspicious. He especially didn't understand why she was still dropping the baby off at an expensive daycare facility every day. After all, now that he was home most of the time, they should easily be able to share child-rearing duties and look after the infant themselves.

Piper sneeringly derided his wholly imaginary ability to do anything of the sort, reminding him forcefully of how shamefully little he'd done to help her with the older children when they were babies. And he'd definitely left one-hundred percent of the messier parts of child-rearing either to her or the nanny they'd employed in those days. The fierceness of her counter-argument caused him to temporarily back off on the subject of daycare, but his suspicions had lingered.

She'd taken to looking over her shoulder constantly every time she took some guy back to his place or to some cheap motel, fearing she was being stalked by some private investigator hired by Pierce. Continuing to indulge in promiscuous behavior was a huge risk, one that verged on tempting fate. At some point, if she didn't stop, Pierce would discover what she was doing and at that point all hell would break loose. Her life would get messy fast. She knew that. And yet she hadn't been able to stop pursuing and bedding men. It was like an addiction, one she was incapable of freeing herself from.

In recent weeks, she'd reached the point of beginning to crack from the pressure. She became more short-tempered and less willing to put up with Pierce's endless questions regarding her daily activities. This further fueled his suspicions and inevitably led to the tension between them becoming unbearable. Piper decided she'd had enough. She wanted out of the marriage, craved nothing more than total freedom to live her life as she saw fit. To fuck whoever she wanted whenever she wanted and never again spend one second worrying about the possible consequences.

Undoubtedly sensing the fragile nature of their union, Pierce badgered his family into taking this trip. In retrospect, she should've put her foot down and announced her intent to separate from him right there and then. She considered it at the time, but hesitated because it wasn't something she wanted to do so abruptly in front of her children. And now she'd learned a terrible lesson in how fragile life really was. Pierce would still be alive right now if she hadn't sought to delay that moment of familial trauma a little longer.

But Pierce wasn't alive anymore.

He was dead over there on the floor by the door, the front of his shirt soaked in blood from where he'd been stabbed in the gut and throat multiple times. Every glimpse of his unmoving form was like a knife through her heart. She was surprised by how much his death pained her now, in light of all the bad feelings and how distant they had become from each other over the years. They'd shared a life together. Brought kids into the world. There were lots of good memories that still meant something, even now. Now that he was gone, she felt like she was missing a part of herself.

She had no clue what had become of Rory and the baby, but there was no sign of them anywhere in the part of the cabin she could see. Nor had she heard any cries from Vance since shaking off the effects of the tranquilizer. She chose to interpret these things as good news. Rory might have gotten away somehow, perhaps with Vance in tow. She hoped this was true. Prayed for it. Not being at all religious, she wasn't normally the praying type, but she felt compelled to do so now. Maybe it would help. Who knew?

She could hope so anyway.

It was pretty much all she had at this point.

She couldn't comfort or otherwise come to the aid of the only one of her children she knew for a fact was still alive. Piper's hands were wrapped so thoroughly in duct tape they felt encased in cement. She couldn't move them at all. Her ankles had also been painstakingly wrapped in tape. Movement wasn't possible. The idea of escape was laughable. She became increasingly distraught at the knowledge of how completely helpless she was. She wished she could talk to her daughter and tell her everything would be okay. Tell her she didn't need to feed bad about getting pregnant. Tell her she was a good girl and that her mother loved her no matter what.

She turned her head to the side and watched as the naked man kneeling next to Kelsey tugged at her navel piercing and grinned at the way this made her squeal. The leering creep had removed the nail from her face, but it was clear he'd not done so in any attempt to allay her suffering.

Quite the opposite, if anything.

Above all else, he clearly wished to prolong her suffering as long as possible. He was an evil man. A devil. And to make it all worse, she knew him. As a young child and as a teenager, his branch of the Weatherby clan had still been somewhat closely involved with Pierce's branch. At some point, though she never knew why exactly, whatever held those relationships together sort of fell away. More than a decade had gone by since she'd last set eyes on the boy she used to catch staring at her so often at those long ago family gatherings.

She wished she could've gone the rest of her life without ever again seeing his face, which was the face of a monster hiding beneath a veneer of handsomeness. A genuine wolf in sheep's clothing.

Her daughter trembled and cried as the monster began to lightly glide his fingers over her flat stomach.

"Don't hurt me," Kelsey told him, her voice small and terrified.

The monster chuckled and said nothing.

His fingers continued to move lightly over her stomach, drifting lower with each slow circle.

Piper lifted her head and glared at the monster.

I'm going to kill you, she thought. *So help me, if I get even half a chance, I'm going to fucking kill you.*

22

THIS TIME WHEN LINDSEY WENT into the upstairs bathroom she closed the door behind her and locked it. If she'd done that last time, things would be so different now. Grant wouldn't have caught her in the act of peeking at the naughty photos. The confrontation and fight that followed would not have happened. It was disconcerting to realize everything could change so abruptly, with no warning at all. Until the moment when he saw the pictures and snapped, she'd expected to spend the rest of her life with him.

She no longer saw things working out that way, despite vaguely hinting otherwise before coming up here. Yes, there was significant appeal in the notion of hitting the figurative reset button and returning things to the way they were. Upon further reflection, however, she realized that would not be possible. Their relationship was irretrievably broken. They would never be able to trust each other again.

Okay, so when looked at objectively, this was largely her fault. In a basic and boring black-and-white way. She didn't normally care to look at things through a prism of everyday morality, but in this case she had no choice. Grant was a strict monogamist. He'd never made any secret of that. Married couples had sex with each other and that was that. There was no room for any extracurricular carnal activity.

To her great regret, Lindsey had expressed enthusiastic support for this stance, assuring him she felt precisely the same way. She did this knowing she fully intended to continue fucking other people whenever she felt like it. Regardless, the rift that existed between them now was a direct result of her violating the agreed upon rules of the relationship.

Whatever.

Rules were stupid, anyway.

She looked forward to moving into a new phase of her life significantly less burdened by rules and guidelines about how to properly behave. The freedom awaiting her on the other side of the current situation was an immensely alluring thing indeed, but for now she needed to stay focused on the job at hand. The first part of that would involve torturing and killing the captives. She was not about to be cheated out of that experience. By having Grant assist her in this endeavor, she would lull him into believing everything was okay between them again, when in reality nothing could be further from the truth.

Then, once they were all dead, she would bury a knife in her husband's back first chance she got.

She approached the wash basin and stared at the reflected image of her nude form in the mirror above it, loving the way she looked with blood all over her torso. What she was seeing was the transformation of fantasy into reality. She'd imagined herself bathing in the blood of her victims countless times. Thinking about things like that had always turned her on and this time was no exception.

That's you, she thought, smiling. *That's fucking real.*

She moaned softly as she slid a hand between her legs, stunned to find herself on the brink of orgasm almost as soon as she touched herself. Biting her lip in an effort to hold back loud sounds of ecstasy, she worked furiously at her clit until the first orgasm hit with enough force to make her weak in the knees. She had to grip a corner of the basin to keep from falling over.

Holy shit.

Still trembling from the pleasure, she let out a big breath and laughed. The laughter came from knowing beyond doubt Grant at his best wasn't capable of making her feel as good as she could with her own fingers. Not even close. Now that the decision to permanently remove him from her life—and from life itself—had been made, it was shockingly clear how truly pathetic he was on every level. Even the way he'd indulged all her darkest and most violent bedroom fantasies was nothing special. Guys into being brutally dominated by a hot chick were a dime-a-dozen. They might not all be as physically appealing as Grant, but so what? From here on out, most of them would be disposable.

As in hacked up and tossed into a dumpster.

She laughed at the thought and leaned closer to her reflection.

That's you, she thought again. *Lindsey Elaine Weatherby, the notorious triple murderer.*

A line formed on her brow as she pursed her lips and gave her current kill count a moment's additional thought. Was it truly three lives she'd erased at this point or did the baby count? True, it would eventually die as a result of her act of neglect, but she had not directly caused its death. It was tempting to add its demise to her tally, because her mindset was definitely "the higher, the better", but she soon decided doing so would cheapen what she was trying to accomplish.

When it came to killing, Lindsey didn't want to be just "good for a girl". She didn't want to be the next Aileen Wuornos. As far as Lindsey was concerned, there was nothing particularly interesting about what that plain-faced whore had done. That was grubby, ordinary, boring shit. What she wanted was to be thought of in the same breath as people like Ted Bundy, Jeffrey Dahmer, BTK, or Gary Ridgway, the Green River Killer. Or even Edmund Kemper. Sure, Kemper hadn't killed significantly more people than Wuornos, but his crimes had been much more gruesomely memorable. Also, there was no conceit or arrogance in recognizing that she was about a million times more attractive than Wuornos. It was her hope that one day far down the line, long after her killing career was over and her crimes had been exposed, her looks alone would help propel her to the highest ranks of notorious killers.

Sex sells, as the old saying went. And her sex appeal factor was off the fucking charts. Guys everywhere would worship her. Of course, many of them would be the weird, creepy type, but so what? They'd drool over her pictures on the true crime websites. Masturbate to them, even.

All that, however, would hopefully happen in the far-off future. She was hoping for a solid decade of killing before her eventual apprehension, possibly even double that if she got good enough at eluding authorities. Spending her later years in jail was something she'd be able to tolerate if she first got to spend the remainder of her youth and perhaps even some of her middle-aged years doing many terrible, awful things to lots of people.

Three was a nice number. A good start. If things worked out the way she expected, she'd get to double it by sunrise tomorrow.

She would get started on that soon enough.

For now, she wanted to get in the shower, wash the coagulating blood from her body, and masturbate again.

She went to the tub and turned on the water until it was as hot as she could stand. Then she stepped under the blistering stream and pulled the curtain closed. As the water sluiced the blood away from her skin and turned the bottom of the tub dark crimson, she again touched her pussy. She gasped in pleasure as her hand began to work faster.

Many vivid, pleasurable images filled her head.

She came again when she pictured burying the claw end of a hammer in the top of Grant's skull.

23

GRANT WAS STILL LYING ON the floor next to the naked, sputtering girl when he heard the stairs start to creak. He turned his head in that direction and saw Lindsey as she was beginning her descent to the first floor. Her body was clean now, flesh glowing after a fresh scrubbing under hot water. She'd chosen to remain nude, just as she said she would prior to heading upstairs. Her still-wet blond hair was combed back from her face, with strands of it adhering to her slender shoulders. There was something almost regal in the way she held her chin up as she came down the stairs

She looked above-it-all. Superior to everyone.

Like a majestic goddess of old descending the steps of a pyramid. He knew some of this impression was attributable to the hyper-adrenalized nature of the evening's activities. All his senses and perceptions seemed heightened. He also knew, however, that Lindsey was a genuinely fantastic-looking woman. She smiled when she looked at him and saw the appreciation in his eyes. There was more than a hint of smugness in the curvature of that lovely mouth.

He felt a pang of sorrow as he reminded himself he would soon have to kill her. It really was a rotten shame in many ways. Women like her didn't come along every day. Or ever, really, at least in his experience.

He had no choice, though.

The bond between them was broken and could not be mended. Not only that, they were each acutely aware of it. Both knew only one of them would leave this place alive. And so they would now engage in a peculiar dance in which they would pretend everything was okay while awaiting the right moment to pounce.

A swift, preemptive strike against her would probably be the safest and smartest way to go, especially now that he'd seen how ruthless she could be. Do it now, right away, while she wasn't expecting it.

It occurred to him what a vulnerable position he was in down here on the floor. He was closer to the girl, their bodies touching, and he had a hand resting on her inner thigh, inches away from her vagina. He was enjoying the way her flesh wouldn't stop trembling beneath his touch. She was mewling continuously and begging him not to do anything "bad" to her. Not that her pleas meant anything to him. Now that the brief episode of melancholy had passed, he was planning to do many extremely bad things to her. The anticipation of it all was wonderful. Unfortunately, it would be stupid to let Lindsey get close to him while he was still on the floor.

He got to his feet and kept his eyes on Lindsey as she passed through the living area with its furniture and blank TV screen on the wall, backing off and putting a few extra feet between them as she came into the blood-spattered dining space.

She was standing next to the girl now, peering down at her with an amused expression for a moment before lifting her chin to look directly at Grant. "You took the nail out of her face."

He shrugged. "She was gagging, choking on her blood."

Lindsey laughed.

Grant had heard his wife laugh probably thousands of times. This laughter was tinged with something different, though. This time he perceived some of that same smug quality he'd detected in her smile as she came down the stairs. He knew what that meant. She thought she was smarter than him. More clever than him. She had total confidence in her ability to outwit him and be the one still alive come daybreak tomorrow. Which was kind of rich, considering how careless she'd been in looking at her pictures earlier.

You won't outsmart me, bitch. I promise you that.

The vow went unspoken. No point in setting things off prematurely. The right moment would come. He had to be patient.

"You're such a humanitarian, Grant. So empathetic and merciful." Another smug chuckle. "It's really kind of pointless, though, don't you think? This girl dies tonight no matter what."

Grant frowned. "I know that. Jesus. Of course I do. I just didn't want her to die yet, that's all."

Lindsey smiled. "Because some of the things you want to do would be more fun with her still around to properly appreciate them."

"Yeah. Exactly."

Lindsey pursed her lips, making a contemplative sound. "I get that. Absolutely. But you really shouldn't limit your options here. Use your imagination. Open up your mind and let that inner sick freak out."

Grant sighed in exasperation. "Well, obviously I'm planning to rape the shit out of her. What, that's not sick enough for you?"

"It's a good start, I guess, but let me ask you this. Have you considered necrophilia?"

Grant gaped at her a moment before shaking his head. "Um . . . no. I mean . . . that's just kind of . . . gross. Sticking my dick in something dead. I don't think I could do that."

Lindsey rolled her eyes. "Pussy."

Grant sneered. "Fuck you. I think I've proven I'm not a goddamn pussy."

His wife seemed unfazed by the anger in his voice. She was still smiling in an almost serene way when she said, "I admit, you've shown a little more balls tonight than I expected, but that's not enough. You've got to be willing to do the things that make you stand out from the crowd. Any ordinary schmuck can kill somebody, but not everybody can be a Ted Bundy or a Jeffrey Dahmer. Those guys were corpse-fuckers, and they're legends. So tell me, Grant—do you want to be a nobody, an ordinary nothing, or do you want to be a fucking legend?"

Grant stared at her in silence for an extended period. Then he shook his head and said, "You are one sick bitch. You know that, right?"

She nodded. "I do. Proud of it, too. You know what you could do, actually? Do a half-and-half kind of thing. Stick your dick in her while she's still alive. Then, while you're going at it, I can cut her throat and let you finish inside her after she's gone."

Another extended, uncomfortable silence ensued.

It was broken when Lindsey put a cupped hand to her mouth and giggled like a schoolgirl.

Grant had no interest in doing as she suggested for several reasons, not the least of which was it would again put him in a distinctly vulnerable position. She might even put the knife in his neck before doing anything to the girl. He almost laughed at the hint of slight uncertainty in this thought. If he was dumb enough to go along with the scenario she described, she would definitely stab the living shit out of him.

Nope. Not gonna happen.

In an effort to distract her from the idea, he said, "She's pregnant, by the way."

Lindsey did an amused double-take upon hearing this news. "Is she? Hmm. How interesting."

There was a malicious glint in her eyes as her gaze again shifted to the girl, who looked up at her with a hopeful look on her face. Seeing it, Grant almost felt sorry for her. *Almost* definitely being the key word here. If the girl was hoping for mercy due to her condition, she was tragically misguided. His distraction gambit had worked, though, and he was grateful Lindsey's attention was focused elsewhere for the moment.

"Hi there. Tell me something, sweetie. Is my man telling the truth? Are you preggers?"

The girl coughed weakly and a few blood-flecked bits of spittle appeared at the corners of her mouth. She sniffled and said, "Yes. Please. I want to live and have my baby. I'll do anything."

Lindsey arched an eyebrow. "Is that so? You really mean that?"

The girl whimpered as she shifted uncomfortably on the floor. "Yes, anything at all. I fucking swear to God."

Lindsey struck a thoughtful pose while stroking her chin. "This is good to know. What did you say your name was, girl?"

Another pitiful whimper. "Kelsey."

Lindsey smirked. "Nice name. Rhymes with mine. Isn't that cute?" She giggled. "It's a nice name for a privileged rich twat, that is. I mean, that's what you are, right? A spoiled cunt who's never had to work a day in her life. Come on, tell me I'm wrong."

The girl's face was blotchy from all the crying, the endless flow of tears smearing her makeup and leaving dark smudges around her eyes that made her look like a reject from a '70s glam rock band.

She exhaled a shuddery breath and said, "I'm a good person."

Lindsey made a tsk-tsk sound and shook her head. "That's a fucking lie and you know it. Good girls don't get knocked up before they've even moved out on their own, which you obviously haven't. But, hey, that's just my opinion. You said you'd do anything to live. Well, let's put that to the test. I have something in mind. It's a big thing to ask of anybody. I mean, *seriously* big. A lot of people, *good* people, would never agree to it no matter the consequences. But if you do it, I promise we'll let you live."

Kelsey's tears abruptly dried up. She looked up at Lindsey in a steadier way now and there was conviction in her voice when she said, "There's nothing I wouldn't do to stay alive."

"You sound like you mean that."

"Tell me what to do and I'll fucking do it. Anything. I mean it."

Lindsey smiled in an insidiously seductive way that sent a shiver down Grant's spine. The girl, Kelsey, didn't know her like he did, because otherwise one glimpse of that smile would be all she needed to dissuade her from entering into any kind of arrangement with Lindsey. He could tell the girl that lying came as easily to his wife as breathing, but what was the point? Either way, she would die. What Lindsey said was one thing, what she'd actually do with this girl was another.

"That's awesome, Kelsey. Seriously. Because what I have in mind is some fucked-up next-level shit like you've never heard of before. If you really go through with it, you'll be my hero for-fucking-ever." Her big smile slowly faded. In a few moments, her expression was as hard and unforgiving as any Grant had ever seen from her. "But there's something else that has to be dealt with first. There's nothing in this world that comes for free, after all."

Too late, the girl's expression turned apprehensive. "What do you mean?"

The woman standing over her was evil incarnate.

Surely she could see that now.

A sound almost like a growl emerged from Lindsey's throat. It was a predatory sound, laced with danger and the promise of imminent suffering. "I said I'd let you live if you do what I want you to do. *You*, Kelsey. *Just* you."

The girl appeared to catch on to what Lindsey was insinuating at the last possible second. She opened her mouth to scream just as Lindsey was lifting up her foot. Grant winced in reflexive sympathy as his wife stomped down on the girl's bare stomach with all her might.

More savage stomping ensued. Grant lost count somewhere around ten crushing impacts. The girl ceased her futile efforts to get out of the way after the third stomp only because she was no longer capable of it. Lindsey was in a frenzy, her wet hair flying about and hanging in her face. The look on her face, what he could see of it as she raged and howled like some wild beast, was sheer fury.

She finally stopped and stood there breathing heavily for several moments, her whole body sheened in sweat. When she finally caught her breath, she looked at the girl's mother and grinned. "Think I took care of that little problem for you. No need to thank me."

She laughed.

Grant let out a breath he hadn't known he'd been holding. "Fuck. Just . . . *fuck*."

Lindsey laughed again. "Exactly."

24

THE BRUTALITY OF THESE PEOPLE continued to astonish Jorge. If there was one silver lining to all this madness, at least from his perspective, it was that the insane couple seemed to have forgotten all about him. Temporarily, at least. He was still stuck down here on the floor, bound to the fallen-over chair, but it wasn't like he was hidden away out of sight somewhere. The respite he was currently enjoying was only happening because his captors were more interested in tormenting the newer arrivals to the cabin. That would change eventually, of course, probably as soon as the mother and daughter were dead.

Because regardless of what Lindsey had promised the girl, she would not survive this experience. Any hints or suggestions to the contrary were only the woman toying with her. The horrific stomping incident was proof enough of that. Those were heavy blows delivered with maximum leverage and force, intended to inflict severe injury. He'd be surprised if any fetus growing inside the girl could have survived the assault. And that was just the tip of the iceberg.

The stomping might also have ruptured vital organs. The girl could be dying from internal bleeding right now.

The knowledge pained Jorge, of course, but there was nothing he could do to help her. That one leg of the chair he'd been working at earlier still felt somewhat fragile, but he wouldn't be able to get back to work on it without making a significant amount of noise. Noise would, of course, draw attention back to him and that was the last thing he wanted. He could only hope there might yet be one more time when both maniacs would be out of the room. If that happened, he was determined to make the most of the opportunity. He would focus every bit of his remaining strength and mental energy on snapping that fucking leg free of the rest of the chair. If he could do that, getting entirely free might become at least remotely possible.

He felt like laughing and crying at the same time. His survival depended on a whole lot of mights, maybes, and ifs. Too fucking many of them, probably. In all likelihood, he was still doomed to die here tonight.

He wasn't ready to give up just yet, but that girl dying sooner rather than later would be bad for him. Yes, there was an element of selfishness in his concern for her well-being. He felt bad about that, but it was basic human nature. With her gone, their attention would shift back to him that much sooner.

The painful crick in his neck was getting worse every time he craned his head around for a look at the girl, to the point where it felt like an icepick was being shoved into his neck. It was so bad he was reluctant to take another look, even after allowing himself a few minutes for the pain to fade slightly. Now, however, panic was rising inside him, his need to know if the girl was still alive overriding his fear of the pain. He wished like hell he could tear the tape away from his face and spit out the woman's soiled panties. If he could do that, he wouldn't feel quite so much like he was choking every time he turned his head.

He decided to rest his neck a few extra minutes before trying to take another look at the girl. His mind drifted as he allowed his eyes to flutter shut. Despite his ever-present terror of the situation, he felt tired. He was still in pain from the things that had been done to him, but right now that steady throbbing felt dull and distant. Hazy images from his childhood came into his head. These included sunny memories of his family on vacation somewhere in Florida. He saw his dad in a Hawaiian shirt grilling burgers by the pool at the cheap beachside motel where they stayed that summer.

Jorge wasn't quite fully asleep in those moments, but he was edging dangerously close to it. The dream of bygone days kept pulling him deeper into unconsciousness, with its promise of a soft, comfortable refuge from the hell his waking life had become. It was tempting to let go and sink all the way into that fuzzy, idealized echo of the past. He'd endured so much and couldn't take much more of it. At the same time, another part of his psyche was sounding the alarm, insisting he needed to snap out of it and focus on what was happening. He needed to be awake and ready to seize the chance to save himself when it came.

As the dream continued to linger, he became aware of voices from the here and now intruding. Multiple voices. Two of them belonged to the crazy couple, but there was one other. A female voice. Something in the timbre of it told him it belonged to the young girl. She was talking to their captors in a subdued way, almost in a monotone. His slow return to full wakefulness began with the realization that the tape must have been removed from her mouth. That more vigilant part of his psyche began screaming at him to wake up. Something had changed during his moments of near-sleep. He needed to open his eyes and finally take another look at what was happening over there.

He heard footsteps.

His eyes finally opened when he sensed people looming over him. He looked up and saw three sets of eyes staring down at him.

The girl was still naked, but she'd been freed from her bonds. He saw the sticky tape residue still on her wrists. Gripped in her right hand was a big knife with a serrated blade. It had been wiped clean, but there were still flecks of blood lodged in the serrations. Had to be the same knife Lindsey had used to murder the girl's father. Jorge's brow creased in confusion. It made no sense. Why would they entrust their captive with a weapon?

He was fully awake by the time the couple knelt and worked together to set the chair he was bound to upright again. The girl was hanging back a bit, a few feet away from them, her expression flat but unflinching as she stared at him. He saw blood between her legs and dark bruising to her abdomen. It took only about a second to understand that the blood was evidence of a forced miscarriage. Jorge looked into her eyes and understood he was looking at someone deeply traumatized by what had happened to her but determined to survive.

It was then he remembered Lindsey's promise to let the girl live in exchange for doing anything they asked of her. Jorge still believed it was an empty and cynical promise, but it was clear the girl believed it was the only chance she had. One she meant to take.

He was so focused on the girl he at first paid little attention to what Lindsey was doing. That changed when he felt her tugging at one of his shoes. He frowned as he glanced down and saw she'd already untied the shoe. It came off in the next instant, along with the black sock he'd been wearing. She then shifted slightly sideways and removed his other shoe, tossing it aside. This was only a mildly curious development at first. He was far more worried about the knife and the girl's grimly determined expression.

Then the man handed his wife a hammer and two more of those enormous nails. The same kind Lindsey had shoved into the girl's face not that long ago, a raw-looking wound that was still dribbling blood. Jorge began to scream behind the gag in his mouth when the woman positioned one of the nails above his bare left foot. He tried rocking the chair over as she raised the hammer over her head. He stopped when the man pressed the razor-sharp blade of a box-cutter to his throat and told him what would happen if he didn't stay still.

Jorge stopped rocking the chair. Terror again engulfed him as tears spilled down his face and all his hopes of escape vanished. The woman looked up at him and smiled in a leering way.

Then she brought the hammer down and the thick length of un-forgiving steel punched through bone and tissue.

25

THE CRAZY BITCH HAD AN eager look on her face. She'd just finished describing for Kelsey what she wanted her to do. In great and hideous detail. There was some small satisfaction when that expectant expression gave way to a look of surprise a moment later. The woman had clearly anticipated anything other than immediate agreement. Loud protestations of disgust, perhaps even refusal to go along with something so vile, because vile it definitely was.

Vile and fucking deranged.

Kelsey had known she would be required to do something awful beyond anything she'd ever imagined. She'd been somewhat mentally prepared for that, but the sadistic scenario conceived by the crazy woman far exceeded her worst fears about what she'd be compelled into doing. And yet she didn't hesitate to say yes. Not even for a second.

Because more than anything in the world, Kelsey Weatherby still wanted to live. She wasn't naive. There was no reason to believe the crazy cunt had any intention of keeping her promise, if for no other reason than because she was a witness to murder and therefore a liability.

In their place, there was no way she'd keep her word, but she'd not abandoned hope yet. She believed there was only one possible path to survival. It did not involve trying to outwit her captors or possibly trying to assault them during a perceived moment of vulnerability. There were two of them and only one of her. If she decided to fight, she might get one of them, but the other one would probably get her. Besides that, they were too guarded, too careful about how they were handling her for any such moment of vulnerability to arise.

The one possible way out was to sink all the way down to their putrid, demented level. She had to be as willing to wallow in utter depravity as they were. More than that. She needed to exceed their warped expectations in every way. To maybe even go beyond what the woman had asked of her. To so impress them with her apparent enjoyment of the evil deed that they might consider her a kindred soul. She might even suggest they take her with them when they left this place, become a trio of traveling killers. Possibly they'd scoff at the notion, but she intended to sell it as hard as she could, because she believed if all went right, they might actually go for it. And then, somewhere out there on the road, she'd figure out a way to get away from them.

There was a lot still ahead of her before that could happen, though. The hardest part of it would be maintaining an outward air of emotionless calm, whereas on the inside she was in a state of extreme anguish. Her father was dead. Her brothers were dead. The life she'd only just learned she was carrying inside her had been stomped out of existence. She could feel what was left of it trickling down her legs after they cut away the tape and allowed her to get to her feet. Her stomach was cramping and other things didn't feel right inside her. She was terrified of what other damage the woman's assault might've inflicted. All that had to be pushed aside. She had to summon levels of physical and mental strength she wasn't sure she possessed.

She might fail.

But she would try her fucking damnedest.

As she stood up, she glanced at her mother and forced herself not to wince at the miserable, beseeching expression on her face.

You have to be hard, she told herself. *Hard and merciless.*

It was the only way.

She sneered at the woman who'd given her life, an expression conveying a level of contempt that wasn't entirely an act. "I have to do it. It's my only chance. I might've said no if you'd been more like a real mother to us, you know. Half the damn town knew you were screwing around on Dad. Except Dad, I guess, and now he'll never know."

Kelsey spat in her mother's face.

The crazy couple gasped in disbelief. Then the woman laughed.

Kelsey worked hard to keep her face blank.

So far, so good.

She helped her captors get her mother off the floor and into a chair. They positioned the chair near the cluttered table, facing the door. For some reason that was not yet clear, the woman was removing Piper Weatherby's shoes. The other man, the one bound to the chair, was still on the floor. He was snoring softly, oblivious to the world of pain about to consume him. She was supposed to do him first, then her mother, but the couple did not appear to be in any huge rush. They were taking their time, enjoying the buildup to the main event.

Kelsey, however, just wanted to get on with it. She'd psyched herself up to doing this horrendous thing, but she wasn't at all sure how long she could keep it together. The sooner they could get started, the better. She wanted it done and behind her. The guilt and trauma that would inevitably follow could wait . . . if she lived.

She made eye contact with the crazy woman as she got to her

feet and set the shoes on the table. "I have an idea. Something to make it even better. But I need one of you to get my bag and my mom's bag from our car. There's some stuff I need in them."

She described the bags for them.

The man and woman exchanged wary, perplexed glances. When the woman looked at her again, her expression was mildly distrustful. "Why do you need them?"

Kelsey told her.

The woman did a double-take. She looked even more surprised than when Kelsey had agreed to do this. "Are you shitting me?"

Kelsey was stone-faced as she said, "No."

Inside, her soul was on fire. She was probably going to hell just for having thought of it. What she'd been asked to do was sickening enough in its own right, but this twist she'd come up with on her own represented a drastic escalation in sheer depravity they'd obviously never even considered. She could tell they were impressed and felt a reflexive twinge of twisted pride despite the deep revulsion she felt for the whole thing.

The woman shook her head and glanced at her husband. "Go get the bags. I'll keep an eye on her."

The man took one step toward the door, but hesitated, eyeing Kelsey suspiciously a moment before again looking at his wife. "Are you sure about that? I don't think we can trust her yet. Maybe you should get the bags while I watch her."

The woman snorted and rolled her eyes. "Why, because you're the man and therefore more capable of keeping her in check?"

The man shrugged. "Well, yeah. Now that you mention it."

The woman scowled at him. "Go get the fucking bags, asshole. I can handle her."

The man grunted. "Whatever."

But he finally started toward the door again. He was still naked as he went outside. Any other time, this would've struck Kelsey as odd, but not on this night. Besides, as isolated as the cabin was, it wasn't like he had to worry about being seen.

Kelsey managed a small, inscrutable smile when he was gone. "Trouble in paradise?"

"You could say that, I guess."

Kelsey fought to keep her smile from widening. This was good shit to know. One more thing she might use against them before it was all over. They'd been angry with each other before, after fucking right in front of her, but now she knew their problems ran deeper than an isolated incident of sexual frustration.

The woman came toward her.

Kelsey needed every ounce of will she had to not immediately retreat or visibly tremble. In another moment, the woman was standing right in front of her. She felt terror and anger. A great urge to smash her in the face rose up inside her. Yet she made herself remain still, keeping her eyes downcast rather than maintaining eye contact.

Sensing her inner struggle, the woman laughed softly. "Relax. I'm not going to hurt you."

She slid a hand between Kelsey's legs and put her mouth close to her ear.

"I want to have a little taste of what I took from you."

Kelsey gritted her teeth and forced herself to remain rigidly still while it happened.

26

GRANT CAME BACK INTO THE cabin with two medium-sized nylon travel bags, one light blue and the other a dark shade of maroon. He carried them over to the table and set them on its already crowded surface after pushing some stuff aside to make room. Lindsey shooed him aside and opened each bag, quickly rifling through the contents to confirm there were no hidden weapons.

There were none.

Clothing items made up the majority of what each bag contained. There were also books, makeup compacts, and clear bags containing toiletries. The blue bag had a cross-stitch kit zipped inside one of the side compartments. Based on what Kelsey had already told them, its presence there confirmed the bag as belonging to her mother, something Lindsey would've been able to figure out anyway. The clothes in the bag were the sort more typically worn by an older woman than a teenager, with the opposite true of the other bag's contents.

Once Lindsey had given her the okay, Kelsey took a moment to go through her own bag, extracting a small plastic packet containing white powder that had been hidden in a rolled-up pair of socks.

Lindsey frowned. "Is that what I think it is?"

Kelsey opened the packet and scooped a bit of the powder out with a fingernail. "If you think it's cocaine, then yes, it is."

She held the powder to a nostril and snorted it up. Another small scoop of powder then went up her other nostril.

Lindsey still felt slightly bewildered. "How does a kid afford cocaine?"

Kelsey smirked. "There's all sorts of ways of getting things. People give me stuff because I'm rich and pretty, especially if they think I'll fuck them. Honestly, I could afford it with the allowance Daddy gives me, or used to give me until you killed him, but it's much more fun getting things for free."

She took yet another small hit of coke.

Lindsey glanced over at Grant, saw the avid way he was observing the girl. She could see his interest in her was close to obsession. Everything about her fascinated him. Her body, of course, which was lovely, admittedly, but also the demeanor she'd exhibited since being freed of her bonds. She was smart and sarcastic, even when faced with horrific things that would break many people much older than her. And now she was showing him her bad girl bonafides.

Despite the rupture in their relationship, Lindsey couldn't help feeling a spark of jealousy.

"That's interesting," she said, voice dripping disdain. "Do you think people will still give you things now that your face is fucked up?"

Kelsey took still another hit of coke and shrugged. She sealed the packet and dropped it in her bag before glancing at Lindsey, showing her an unfazed expression. "With all the money I'll be inheriting, I'll be able to afford high-end plastic surgery. I'll be fine. Assuming you honor your word and let me live after I do this, that is."

Lindsey frowned. "I don't lie, bitch."

Grant snorted.

She shot him an angry look. "Got something to say, husband?"

He smiled. "Not at all, dear. You are a paragon of truth and honesty. I'd never suggest otherwise."

The overt sarcasm in his voice pissed Lindsey off. So did the wink he directed at the girl. Her anger was close to boiling over for a moment, but she managed to rein it in, not wanting the girl to believe she could be manipulated to the point of explosion so easily. She was the adult here, goddammit, and the girl was just a kid. The only acceptable option, for now, was to act above it all and project an air of not giving a damn.

Later, of course, both of these shit-stains would face severe consequences.

She rolled her eyes. "Whatever. Let's get on with this shit."

A short conversation about how to proceed ensued. Once everyone was in agreement, things began to happen swiftly. Lindsey fetched a clean silver baking pan from the kitchen. She set the pan on the table and returned to the kitchen to clean the knife the girl would be using, wiping the blade off with a paper towel after running it under hot water for a minute.

The next part was fun.

After setting the snoozing brown-skinned man upright in his chair again, Lindsey went to work with the nails. The thrill that went through her as she pounded them through his feet and deep into the floor was electric. His screams were a wicked delight. This was the shit she'd gotten into this for. The joy of torturing another human being. It was so intoxicating she decided to forego making the girl nail her mother's feet to the floor. She would do it herself and enjoy another dose of pure, uncut human misery, a high she was certain was far more exhilarating than anything the girl's narcotics could deliver.

The mother's screams as Lindsey pounded the big nails into her feet were so loud and so shrill it was like having your eardrums perforated by a dentist's drill. After banging home the last nail, Lindsey glanced at the girl and was pleased by the way her face had turned deathly pale. She seemed a lot less defiant and a lot more vulnerable than she had only a few minutes ago.

Kelsey had been hovering meekly in the background as all this happened, but now it was showtime.

Lindsey smacked her ass. "Get to it, bitch."

The girl needed a moment to compose herself.

Then she went to work with the knife.

27

THE PAIN WAS BEYOND ANYTHING Piper had ever imagined. She had small feet. Those big nails had punched through them with shocking, devastating ease. The presence of those thick pieces of steel inside her flesh felt unnatural and obscene. Every tiny twitch of her violated flesh sent more jolts of agony sizzling through her body.

Even worse was the contemplation of what was still to come. She'd come close to sliding into unconsciousness at one point, but she'd heard the bulk of her daughter's horrifying conversation with the crazy couple. Hearing Kelsey agree so readily to do such awful things hurt her in a way that was almost as bad as the physical pain. She'd said such mean things. They were things said under extreme duress, of course, but she'd heard the underlying conviction in her daughter's voice.

Kelsey believed every word of it.

She hated her mother. No, more than that. *Despised* her.

And now she appeared to be going through with the sickening

act she'd agreed to perpetrate in exchange for her life.

Piper turned her head and watched as Kelsey yanked out the screwdriver lodged in the Mexican man's leg and tossed it to the floor. The man howled miserably as the metal came out of his flesh. The man and woman laughed gleefully at this confirmation of his suffering. They were evil beings disguised as humans. Demons. Thinking of it this way was the only way Piper could even begin to process what was happening.

She watched her daughter climb atop the Mexican and straddle him like a stripper giving a lapdance to a junior ad executive. Her late husband's much younger cousin touched his genitals as she did this. A wave of disgust washed through Piper as she watched him fondle himself. The bound man's next scream came as an almost welcome distraction.

The crazy woman was standing behind the screaming man now. She looped her husband's belt around the middle of the man's face and pulled his head backward to keep it still. Kelsey then applied the sharp edge of the big knife to the skin just beneath the man's hairline. She held it there a moment, unmoving as she appeared to hold her breath.

The woman screamed at her, spewing threats.

Kelsey exhaled and began to saw into the man's flesh. Blood immediately began to leak from the initially small incision below his hairline. As the incision widened all the way across his forehead, the blood fell out in a sheet of crimson. The captive screamed and bucked violently in the chair, but Kelsey and the crazy woman managed to keep him in place by working together. The woman was also screaming throughout this, but her screaming was imbued with a mocking quality. Her screams alternated with bursts of wild laughter. Grant Weatherby continued to hang back and watch, his penis stiffening slightly as he tugged at it. He didn't seem quite able to achieve full arousal, at least not yet. It was about the only thing Piper could be grateful for as she continued to watch this horrific spectacle unfold.

Bile rose into Piper's throat as she watched her daughter grip a handful of the bound man's hair and tug it upward. She heard skin tearing as the edge of the man's scalp peeled away from his forehead. Her stomach churned as Kelsey slid the edge of the blade inside the widened gash and began to saw at his flesh again along the side of his head toward the back. The bound man's thrashing became even more frantic. Piper saw the way his feet were jerking against the nails that had been driven into them and knew the pain from that alone must be almost impossible to bear. What Kelsey was doing to his poor head on top of that had to be absolutely hellish.

Piper wanted to close her eyes and pretend none of this was happening. She didn't want to see the daughter she loved so much doing something so evil. She wished she could *unsee* it, erase it from her memory entirely, but wishful thinking was worse than useless in this situation. All she could do was pray for the soul of that poor man. Maybe it wouldn't do any good. She didn't know. Probably it wouldn't. She did it anyway.

Kelsey stood up somewhat straighter while still straddling the man in the chair, almost in a frenzy now as she continued to saw harder and harder at his scalp. Sounds of frantic exertion sprang from her mouth as she at last took the knife away from the man's head, grabbed a handful of his damp hair, and pulled at it as hard as she could. Strands of bloody tissue snapped as the scalp began to peel loose, exposing the skull beneath. Kelsey cried out in triumph as it came all the way free. She held it aloft as she disengaged herself from the man she'd disfigured and stood there breathing heavily for a moment.

The man and woman whooped it up, sounding like football fans celebrating a touchdown. Meanwhile, the man in the chair whimpered and trembled continuously. It struck Piper as particularly horrible that he was still alive after that. He'd probably be better off dead at this point.

Kelsey approached the table and carefully set the bloody scrap of hairy flesh on the silver baking tray. She took a few moments carefully spreading it out and arranging it in a way that was almost loving. Or maybe that was a twisted misperception of her own fracturing psyche, straining to find evidence of something still human inside her daughter.

A moment of unexpected quiet ensued.

The deranged couple's almost identical expressions of maniacal joy faded, yielding to looks that appeared more thoughtful. No one moved or said anything. Piper sat perfectly still despite the awful pain still consuming her. She wished that moment could go on forever, that the personal horror awaiting her could be delayed indefinitely.

Then the moment of pause ended. Again, nothing was said, but Piper felt it like a change in atmospheric pressure. Still without saying a word, the three of them approached her and stood arrayed around her. Kelsey was in front of her with the knife. The crazy woman was behind her with the belt. And Grant was off to the side, cock in hand again as he leered at them.

Kelsey's expression was flat as she said, "It's your turn, Mom."

Not *I'm sorry* or *I wish I didn't have to do this.*

Just *It's your turn.*

All syllables uttered without a flicker of detectable emotion.

The crazy woman looped the belt around her face, pulling the leather taut over her eyes.

Then Kelsey applied the blade to her mother's hairline and began to cut.

28

HAVING SUCCESSFULLY REMOVED ONE HUMAN scalp already, Kelsey had a better idea of how to efficiently perform the procedure when the time came to do the same thing to her mother. This was a good thing, because above all else, she wanted it done quickly, hopefully in no more than about a minute or two. She reckoned that would be about half the time she'd needed to get the Hispanic man's scalp off his head.

She had lots of issues with her mother. Both of her parents had been sort of absent and inattentive, especially over the last several years. Her father had been trying to change that recently, but even before he died it'd been a case of too little, too late. The family was too dysfunctional to fix, at least not without a lot of years of therapy. Which would never happen now.

The bitterness she felt toward her parents did not, however, mean she didn't love them. She did now and always had, though she often wavered regarding which of them she sympathized with more. That was not the case now. Her father was dead and no longer part of the equation, whereas her mother was still alive, albeit likely not for much longer. Despite the terrible things Kelsey had said to her to impress the crazy couple, she didn't wish to cause her more pain than was absolutely necessary to get the job done.

She worked even faster than she'd hoped, cutting and tearing away her mother's scalp in barely more than a minute. As she worked with the knife, she clenched her teeth tight and made a loud, continuous grunting sound in an effort to distract herself from her mother's desperate screaming. She felt queasy upon glimpsing the exposed top of her skull and immediately reeled away from her. Choking back the vomit her stomach was trying to expel wasn't easy, but she managed to do it as sweat broke out on her brow.

The crazy man and woman were watching her closely with an obvious air of expectation. She could tell they were waiting for her to break, believing it inevitable. Well, she wouldn't give them the satisfaction. Instead of being sick all over the floor, she again held the scalp aloft and made a sound of primal triumph, as if she were some sort of savage cannibal woman of the jungle. Those expectant, leering looks again gave way to smiles and nods of approval. The guy especially looked pleased. He winked at her again and she smiled in return. The beginnings of an idea were coalescing in her head. She thought she might be able to seduce the perv and turn him against his woman, maybe even goad him into killing her.

The woman wasn't stupid, though. Far from it. She was probably the sharper of the two by a wide margin. Kelsey was no psychic. She couldn't know the inner thoughts of either of these fucking maniacs, but she had a clear sense the woman was already worried about the possibility of her husband turning against her and hooking up with their young captive.

Bitch was right to be worried.

Kelsey definitely meant to strike fast and kill the woman when the right moment came. It would happen as soon as she was certain she could attempt it without fear of retribution from the husband.

She carried her mother's scalp over to the table and set it on the silver baking tray, after which she spent some moments arranging the long blood-streaked blond locks attached to the flap of flesh she'd carved off her mother's head. As she did this, she listened to the screams and whimpers of her mother and the other man. The sounds were nonstop. They grated on her nerves and she had some moments where she wished more than anything she could silence them. Just suddenly cut their throats in an act of mercy and spare them the horror of what was still to come.

She couldn't do that, though.

It would go against the prolonged exercise in sadistic cruelty she'd promised her captors. Her victims needed to be alive for it. This was a core component of what she'd described while making her pitch to them. Even the guy might turn against her if she failed to deliver, and she was determined not to lose the headway she'd made with him. Her life probably depended on it.

Kelsey opened the box containing her mother's cross-stitch kit, removing and setting aside a square of white fabric and a wooden hoop. Next she removed the needle and several packets of thread, all different colors. She opened a packet of blue thread, licked the end of it, and fed it through the eye of the needle, neatly tying it off.

Her mother wasn't really a cross-stitch kind of person, but Piper Weatherby had some leftover supplies that had belonged to *her* mother, who'd succumbed to cancer a few years back. She occasionally made half-hearted attempts to get into it, but didn't really have the patience for it. Prior to leaving on their doomed excursion to the cabin, she'd impulsively announced her intent to try again while they were away.

Kelsey, however, had been a natural cross-stitcher as a young child, learning quickly under the guidance of her late grandmother. She and her brother had spent two weeks with their grandparents every summer back in those days, while their parents went on extended trips to exotic locations around the world without them. She guessed her parents had actually still been truly in love with each other back then, which was weird to think about now after the years of apparent indifference.

Once she had the needle and thread ready, she grabbed a handful of her mother's blond hair, lifted the scalp off the tray, and carried it over to where the Hispanic man remained bound to the chair. She straddled him again and waited a moment while the woman again looped the belt around his face to keep his head from moving too much.

She then carefully set her mother's scalp atop the trembling man's exposed skull, smoothing it into place as best she could. It wasn't a perfect fit. Of course not. Their heads were different sizes. But she did the best she could. Perfect wasn't even really necessary. She was hoping to get it so it would remain functionally attached for at least a short while. Long enough for these lunatics to have their fun and be satisfied by what she'd done for them.

When she was satisfied with the placement, she lifted up her mother's hair on one side and used a bobby pin to clip it in place. This would allow her to begin the transplant relatively unimpeded.

The man started screaming again when she pressed the tip of the needle to the line of bloody skin below the exposed top of his skull. She pushed the needle through the skin, felt it touch the skull, and then angled it upward, pulling needle and thread all the way through until she had several inches of slack thread with which to work. Next she lifted up the edge of her mother's scalp and pushed the needle through the slippery, bloody flesh. Keeping a firm enough grip on it to work efficiently wasn't easy, but she did her best. The man bucking against her didn't help matters any, but at least it wasn't quite as much like riding a wild bronco this time. She guessed his strength was fading some, which she supposed was to be expected.

Once she'd made the first few connecting stitches, it got easier. The crazy man and woman kept giggling and making sounds of amused astonishment. For the time being at least, the woman seemed so impressed she'd at least temporarily set aside her burgeoning resentment and suspicion of Kelsey.

The frayed line of skin at the base of the man's skull was stretched tighter now as a result of her work with the needle and thread. She had to use her long fingernails to peel it back from the skull and resume the stitching job. After another several stitches, she paused to undo the pinned-up hair and smooth it down the side where the stitching was already complete. She then lifted the hair on the other side of the man's head and used the bobby pin to clip it in place. More peeling and stretching of skin was required to complete the job, but by then she had such a feel for what she was doing that it had become disturbingly easy.

At last, after what felt like a lifetime in hell, she was finished. Her mother's scalp had been firmly sewn into place on another human being's head. She unclipped the hair pinned up atop the man's head, smoothed it down, and eased herself off the whimpering captive. Though she felt disgust for this terrible thing she'd done, she took some moments to study her work and appraise its quality. Given the tools at her disposal, she believed she'd done the best possible job a person with zero surgical training could do. Even so, on a purely visual level, the result was something that looked both ridiculous and horribly surreal. Her mother's salon-styled hair was heavily flecked with blood, but the long blond locks looked absurdly out of place attached to this burly guy.

The crazy man and woman were laughing hysterically.

To her dismay, Kelsey found she could understand why they were so amused. A small smile tugged at the corners of her mouth. She made it go away as another surge of self-disgust rose up inside her. What kind of person would commit this kind of atrocity to save their own skin?

But she already knew the answer to that.

A bad one.

She flinched when music started playing. Some loud rock song from long before she was born, she guessed. The band and song were unknown to her, but the title was pretty easy to figure out from the chorus: "Dude Looks Like A Lady."

Kelsey couldn't help it.

She started giggling.

29

LINDSEY WONDERED WHAT GRANT WAS up to when he moved to retrieve his pants from the floor, frowning even in the midst of her laughter. She was still standing behind the bound man, but the girl was nearly finished with her stitching job and so her assistance was no longer needed. She took the belt away from the man's face and held it by one end, with the buckle dangling toward the floor. She would use the belt as a makeshift weapon if necessary, whipping the buckle across her husband's face if she sensed he was about to make any kind of move against her. Because such a move was coming sooner or later. The only question was who would try something first.

She sighed in relief when he let his jeans fall again to the floor and saw he was holding his phone. He tapped the screen and started scrolling. Again, she wondered what he was up to, but the answer came seconds later when music began emanating from the phone. The song was one she knew from her days of hanging out in dive bars in college. Oldies dominated the jukeboxes in some of those places. She started laughing again as soon as she recognized it.

It was perfect.

Even the girl started giggling, which was surprising. She had powered through the gruesome task assigned to her with grim determination, and without once breaking down or botching the job. From her position behind the chair, however, Lindsey had been able to closely study the girl's face and sensed how fragile her composure was. She was working hard to keep it together long enough to finish attaching her mother's scalp to the head of the Hispanic man. In the end, she got it done, but it clearly took a huge mental toll on her. It'd be interesting to see whether she'd be able to maintain a similar level of composure while attaching the Hispanic man's scalp to her mother's head.

Grant was dancing in the dorkiest way imaginable, bopping his way back over to this side of the table and belting out his own off-key version of the song's chorus. Lindsey's feelings where he was concerned had taken a permanent turn toward the negative in the wake of the bathroom assault, but she couldn't help feeling a certain amused warmth for him as she watched the ridiculous display. The way his dick and balls flapped around as he danced only added to the hilarity.

Getting into the spirit of the moment, Lindsey started dancing, too. Maintaining her grip on the belt, she came out from behind the chair and started wiggling her ass at the bound man. His continuous whimpering was still audible above the music. Inspiration struck. She plopped down on his lap and started grinding away at his crotch.

She made eye contact with Grant and smiled. "Record me."

Grinning, he aimed his phone at her, tapped its screen, and continued dancing, albeit in a more restrained way as he sought to document Lindsey's performance. "It looks like you're giving the world's ugliest woman a lap dance. It's sort of hot. In a weird way."

Lindsey laughed as the song came to an end. "Put on something else. Some kind of stripper song."

Grant tapped the screen a few more times.

When "Take If Off" by Kesha started playing, Lindsey's dancing became much more animated. She bounced up off their captive's lap, spun around, and plopped down atop him again. This time she was straddling him as she continued to grind away at him. Grant kept the phone aimed at her as he moved off to the side to capture it all from a better angle.

Lindsey glanced over at the girl to verify she wasn't seeking to take advantage of their divided attention. The girl saw her watching, wincing slightly as they made eye contact. Lindsey yelled out to her, pitching her voice high enough to be heard over the music as she warned the girl against doing anything that might get her hurt. She also told her to come closer and get away from the table, a command she instantly obeyed.

Satisfied she wasn't an immediate threat, Lindsey focused again on the man trembling and whimpering beneath her. She knew he was too traumatized and in too much pain to derive any pleasure from her erotic dance, but she wasn't doing it for him. The recording was something she planned to enjoy many times later on, after she fled the country and this crazy night was in the past.

She raised her torso and rubbed her breasts against the man's face, a move that elicited a whistle of appreciation from Grant. The dance continued even after the Kesha song ended. At her direction, Grant picked out something else, some slow hip-hop track she didn't know. She'd shifted positions against the bound man multiple times throughout the dance, but now she straddled him again and looped the belt around his neck, feeding the end of it through the buckle and pulling it tight while slowly grinding against him in time to the music. His eyes bulged open as she pulled it even tighter. He began to struggle weakly again as pitiful wheezing sounds emanated from his throat.

Grant moved in closer, his voice becoming huskier as he said,

"Do it, baby, do it. Finish him off."

Lindsey stopped grinding and looked at the phone. "No. It's not time for that. Turn the fucking music off."

Grant frowned as he tapped the phone's screen, silencing the music. "Damn. I was enjoying that. I love how twisted you are."

Lindsey considered reminding him how he hadn't seemed so certain on that count not so long ago, but she refrained, deciding it was best for now to avoid picking at anything that might get tensions boiling again. Better to lull him into a false sense of comfort and renewed comradery with his wife.

She loosened the belt and took it away from the bound man's throat. At that point, she climbed off him and moved back a few steps. The buckle end of the belt was again dangling toward the floor. Some tense, silent moments elapsed as no one said anything.

Grant cleared his throat. "Um . . . everything okay, Lindsey? You seem a little on edge all of a sudden."

Lindsey almost laughed.

Instead, she turned her head slowly toward him, smiling tightly as she said, "Everything's fine."

She then wheeled about and lashed out with the belt, whipping the buckle across the girl's face.

30

THE PAIN KELSEY FELT WHEN the buckle hit her wasn't the worst she'd experienced tonight, but it was enough to make her shriek in surprise and drop to her knees. Before she could try getting back to her feet, the crazy woman was behind her again, looping the belt around her neck and pulling it tight enough to make her sputter and gasp for breath.

Once the woman had cinched the belt as tight as she could without actually choking her to death, she put a hand on Kelsey's shoulder and pressed down hard to keep her from standing.

Then she put her mouth against Kelsey's ear. "The party's over, you stupid cunt. You still have work to do. Better get to it before I get really mad. Believe me, you don't want that to happen."

She held the belt in place a moment longer, seeming to enjoy Kelsey's desperate struggle to draw in air. Then she took the belt away and gave her a hard kick in the ass, making her crumple to the floor, where she lay gasping for several moments as the woman continued to loudly berate her.

"Get up! Get up, you filthy fucking whore! Lift that scrawny little ass of yours up before I cut your fucking throat!"

Before Kelsey could even attempt to obey this command, the woman kicked her in the side. She moaned in agony and rolled onto her back as pain exploded inside her. The pain from the stomping she'd taken earlier had never come close to going away, but it had subsided to a level where she could manage to function. Well, that was all over now. It again felt like something was wrong inside her, broken or nearly ruptured. Tears streamed from her eyes as she begged the woman not to kick her again. She was terrified of what another kick that ferocious might do. It probably wouldn't kill her—she hoped—but it might hurt enough to make her wish she was dead.

The woman kept screaming at her to get up. There was nothing even faintly resembling mercy or compassion in that voice. Kelsey whimpered and flinched every time the buckle snapped against the floor, close to her head. The woman's burst of rage was so extreme it even seemed to give her husband pause. He suggested she should ease up in a surprisingly meek voice. The woman ignored him and pulled her leg back, ready to kick again.

Kelsey choked back a sob and said, "I'm getting up."

Seeing that leg poised to kick was all the motivation she needed. Rolling over again, she braced her hands on the floor, the muscles in her arms shaking as she struggled to raise herself up. She felt like giving up multiple times, but she kept at it, pushing through in the same grimly determined way that had allowed her to complete the first part of the scalp transplant. Now she needed to call up a similar reserve of strength to see her the rest of the way through this. She wasn't at all certain she could manage it now. It'd taken everything she had to finish the first part. Even before this latest assault, sewing the man's scalp to her mother's head was going to be extraordinarily difficult. She'd been pushed to her limits and far beyond.

And yet she had no choice but to try.

The level of exertion required to get all the way upright again made her scream in pain, but she kept pushing and was finally able to do it. She sniffled and had to fight hard not to descend into a fit of hysterical crying. Wiping the tears from her eyes, she glanced at the woman and felt an intense wave of hatred and anger sweep through her. In that moment, she wanted nothing more than to take a knife and carve the smug look off her fucking face. At the same time, offending the woman was the last thing she wanted, so she tried hard to keep her hatred from showing. Which wasn't really possible, of course. The woman's leering expression showed she knew precisely what Kelsey was feeling and felt nothing but contempt for it.

Kelsey heaved a breath and haltingly approached the table. She walked slightly hunched-over, gently holding a hand to her stomach as sweat poured down her face. She paused as she reached the table, taking some moments to catch her breath.

She expected the woman to start screaming at her again, maybe hit her or whip her with the belt, but that didn't happen. She glanced at the man and woman surreptitiously, without looking directly at either of them. They were watching her in the same expectant way they had earlier, eager to see this next progression of her debasement unfold.

In that moment she more clearly understood there was next to no chance here of any outcome that didn't involve her death. One look at the woman's deranged expression was enough to confirm her true intentions beyond even the slightest doubt. Once again, however, Kelsey chose to press ahead anyway.

She took another packet of thread from the cross-stitch kit and tore the packaging open with her shaking hands. Threading the needle this time took longer because of the shaking. She jabbed her fingers with it multiple times before she managed to get it done.

Just one scalp remained on the blood-smeared baking tray. Before picking it up, she put the needle and thread down and opened the packet of cocaine, again using a long fingernail to scoop out several bumps. She felt steadier and less afraid almost as soon as the drug hit her system. Though she'd already had more than she normally would at one time, she kept at it, snorting it up until the packet was nearly depleted. When she dropped the packet on the table and again picked up needle and thread, her hands were no longer shaking.

She picked up the scalp and approached her mother, who was quietly sobbing and staring at the floor. Her slender shoulders were shaking and without her hair she almost didn't look like her mother at all, an impression enhanced by the mask of coagulating blood obscuring much about her features. When she sensed her daughter's presence, she lifted her head and looked at Kelsey through eyes shimmering with tears. She mumbled something, but in a weaker voice than before, rendering her words impossible to decipher from behind the tape. It was quite a change from earlier, when she'd fought desperately to defend her daughter. Now she sounded broken and defeated, ready to die, something Kelsey supposed was to be expected after being scalped by one's own daughter.

Kelsey had snorted up the bulk of her modest coke supply in an effort to stifle her emotions, because only by doing that would she stand any chance of getting this done. But as she straddled her mother on the chair, an unexpected surge of raw emotion threatened to overwhelm her. She felt queasy and had tears in her eyes as the crazy woman moved into position behind the chair, looped the belt around Piper Weatherby's blood-stained face, and pulled her head roughly backward.

Some moments passed as she struggled to push back the queasiness and contain her emotions. She didn't want to do this to her mother, even now, after she'd done so many horrible things in the name of self-preservation. Making matters worse was the pain and cramping in her abdominal area, which was flaring up again in a big way. She ached to slide to the floor and curl up in a fetal ball. The only reason she didn't was because she knew the woman would interpret this as total failure, giving her the greenlight to resume whipping and stomping her, probably until she was dead.

"Get on with it, bitch," the crazy woman snarled at her from the other side of the chair. She laughed in that mean, sneering way of hers. "Unless you're ready to give up and accept your punishment. It that it, girl? You ready to die now?"

The guy was recording again. He'd moved in close from the side and was aiming the phone at Kelsey's face. "I don't think that's true at all," he said, his tone one of reassurance. "She's stronger than that. Come on, Kelsey, prove her wrong. You've already done some seriously badass shit. You've got this. I know you do."

Kelsey glanced at him, recalling her vague notion of somehow turning him against his wife. That had always seemed an iffy proposition at best and now she was running out of time to find a way to make it happen. The tension between the two of them remained a palpable thing, however, so maybe there was still a chance of swaying him to intercede on her behalf when the woman inevitably decided it was time to kill her.

The woman laughed. "Bullshit. Look at her. She's falling apart."

Kelsey made direct eye contact with the man. When he smiled and winked at her, she swallowed the lump in her throat and blew out a big breath. Feeling slightly calmer, she placed the scalp atop the exposed part of her mother's skull and began the process of smoothing it into place. Because the Hispanic man's head was bigger, the edges of the scalp would significantly overlap the edges of her mother's sliced flesh. Stitching the edges together would require less stretching of the flesh this time, but the fit would be loose and awkward-looking. Telling herself it wouldn't matter as long as she managed to complete the stitching job, she pressed the needle to her mother's flesh and began to push it in. In the same moment, the worst abdominal cramp yet made her stomach feel like it was being turned inside-out. She was utterly powerless to hold back the tide of nausea that rose up inside her like a tsunami.

Vomit exploded from her mouth and struck her mother in the face, hitting her like a stream of water from a firehose. Another powerful wave of nausea came over Kelsey almost immediately. She let go of the scalp and leaned backward slightly, but the second explosive blast of vomit again hit her mother dead-center in the face. If not for the duct tape covering her mouth, a lot of it would've gone straight down her throat.

Her captors made several sounds of disgust as this happened, but they were laughing, too. Both of them. She got a glimpse of the man's face between the eruptions of puke and felt further sickened by his expression of leering amusement. She was crazy to ever have looked at him as anything like a source of comfort or encouragement.

She vomited on her mother's face one more time, but there wasn't as much of it now. Her stomach continued heaving despite having already expelled the entirety of its contents. She felt hot, acidic bile touch the back of her throat and whimpered as tears rolled down her face. At the same time, her mother was trying hard to draw in air through her nostrils. The layer of duct tape over her mouth kept being sucked in and out as her lungs worked overtime. An impulse to rip the tape away was too powerful to resist. She tried peeling at an edge of the tape, but the vomit made it too slippery to grip.

The crazy woman took the belt away from Piper Weatherby's face and started whipping mother and daughter with it. They remained entwined on the chair as the buckle bit into their flesh in numerous places. Kelsey sagged against her mother and sobbed miserably as she listened to the buckle ring against her exposed skull. Unable to take any further abuse, she was ready to give up.

Then the man grabbed hold of her and hauled her off her mother, dumping her on the floor. She rolled onto her back and stared blearily up at the ceiling. Seconds later, the sadistic crazy woman was looming above her, belt still in hand.

She grinned. "Oh, well. Close, but no cigar. Ready to die now?"

Kelsey turned her head to look at the man, imploring him with her eyes before managing to weakly utter a single word: "*Help* . . ."

He no longer had his phone. In its place was a knife, gripped tight in his right hand. Despite everything, Kelsey felt a small spark of hope. Maybe he really *would* help her. Husband and wife stood on opposite sides of her. The woman leered down at her, her grip tightening around the belt. In that moment, she seemed oblivious to her husband, who was staring right at her with a murderous expression.

The crazy woman began to lift the belt.

Her husband's fingers flexed around the handle of the big knife.

And from somewhere right outside the cabin's closed front door came a sound that startled them all—the distressed crying of an infant.

31

THE GIRL COUGHED AND SPUTTERED and tried to sit up as soon as they all heard the squalling of the infant, a sound that seemed to be coming from the general direction of the porch. Her mother also became dramatically more animated upon hearing the sound, bucking against her bonds and straining to tear her feet free of the big nails holding them to the floor.

Grant glanced at her and couldn't help wincing when he saw the head of the nail sink into the flesh beneath the top of her right foot. She was screaming behind the duct tape. The pain had to be beyond unbearable, yet she kept at it. He could scarcely fathom the level of desperation and determination necessary to do something like that. The bottom of the foot was coming off the floor, leaking a steady stream of blood as part of the nail became visible beneath it.

At that point, it was clear she was going to get at least one foot free, and if she could endure the agony that came with doing something that incredible, she'd probably be able to do the same with the other foot, too. As this was happening, Lindsey's gaze was riveted to the closed front door. Her obvious shock at what she was hearing had rendered her oblivious to everything else. If not for that, Grant would've immediately raised the alarm about what the girl's mother was doing. He also still didn't consider the mother anything like a real threat. Even if she managed to get both feet free, she would still be bound to the chair. Even free of the chair and her bonds, she'd still be severely inhibited by her hobbled feet.

He looked at Lindsey. "I thought you killed the fucking baby."

She glanced at him a moment, frowning, before her gaze went back to the door. "I *did*. Sort of."

Grant gasped and sputtered, temporarily befuddled by this statement. "What th—" He gave his head a hard shake and smacked a hand against his forehead, as if to kick his brain back into gear. "I mean, hold on, what the actual fuck do you mean by *sort of?*"

She was gnawing nervously at her bottom lip as she glanced at him again. "Okay, I killed the brother. The older one. He's definitely fucking dead, but I left the baby out there on the private drive. And I mean *way* out there, like hundreds of feet away. There's no way a fucking *infant* could've crawled all the way up here. It makes no sense."

Grant rubbed at his eyes and shook his head again. "Let me be sure I've got this perfectly fucking straight. You left the baby out there . . . *alive?*"

She scowled. "*Yes*, goddammit. Isn't that obvious by now?"

Grant huffed out a breath of utter astonishment. "*Nothing* is fucking obvious anymore. Why would you do that?"

Her defensiveness faded and she looked mildly chagrined as she said, "Because I thought it was this uber-fucking-cold, super-cruel thing to do, leaving it to get dragged off by wolves or a bear or some fucking shit like that."

Grant smirked. "Well, call it a crazy hunch, but I don't think that's what happened."

Lindsey rolled her eyes. "Yes, I know that. *Now*. The question is, what *did* happen?"

Still smirking, he said, "Only one way to find out."

He went to the window by the door and pulled back the curtain to look out at the porch. The porch light was still on from the last time he'd ventured out to the camper. He saw the baby right away, lying on its back on the porch and still swaddled in its blanket. The presence of the blanket told him someone had carried the baby up to the cabin and set him there. While the possibility of the baby crawling all the way up to the cabin on its own struck him as unlikely in the extreme, if that was indeed what *had* happened, surely it would've shed the blanket somewhere along the way.

"Well, there's definitely a fucking baby out there." He turned his head this way and that, scanning the area for signs of an interloper. Nothing. "Don't see anybody else out there, though."

Lindsey frowned. "Do you think it really did make it up here by itself?"

Still staring out at the porch, Grant shook his head. "No, I don't think that."

He explained his reasoning.

Lindsey sighed and conceded that it made sense. "So someone else is out there, even if you can't see them. Hiding."

Grant nodded. "Seems likely."

He sensed his wife's rapidly rising fear of the possibility and all its implications, mirroring as they did what he was also feeling. Glancing back at her, he became conscious again of the knife still in his hand. He thought of how close he'd come to lunging at her with it mere minutes ago. His plan had been to slam the knife into her throat while she was distracted by the prospect of whipping the girl again. It wouldn't have taken her long to bleed out from a wound like that, and killing her would've freed him from the worry of her doing the same to him as soon as she got the chance.

After that, he'd been planning to take the girl with him when he left this place, maybe keep her prisoner in the camper until he had to get out of the country. He figured he needed to be gone from the states and headed somewhere with fuzzy or difficult extradition laws within no more than a day or so. The girl wouldn't be able to flee the country with him, obviously, but that day together would allow him ample opportunity to do all the things he'd been fantasizing about doing to her. He was still hoping for that, but he'd first have to get past the complications presented by this baby and the unseen interloper.

He looked out at the clearing and saw no one lurking in the vicinity of the truck, but that didn't mean much. Part of the problem was the way he'd parked, parallel to the long porch instead of pulling straight up. The attached camper was large enough that someone could easily be hiding between the truck and his dead cousin's minivan. The porch light not being very bright wasn't helpful either. Someone could easily be hanging back in the darkness at the edge of the clearing.

Lindsey made a sound of flustered impatience. "What're we gonna do?"

Grant looked at the baby again. "I don't know. I'm trying to think."

Lindsey grunted. "Great. *Now* you decide to start thinking."

Grant stepped back from the window and turned slowly toward her, glowering as he made eye contact with her. The anger that had been simmering inside him since learning of her cheating ways again threatened to boil over. His grip on the knife's handle tightened again. "Oh, that's rich, coming from you, the fucking genius who ditched our carefully formulated plan almost right from the goddamn beginning. None of this bullshit would be happening if not for you."

Instead of immediately snapping back at him in her usual snide way, Lindsey looked at the knife and frowned at the way his hand was shaking. She'd finally realized how close he was to exploding and seemed ill at ease, perhaps suspecting she wouldn't be able to fend him off with the belt if he took a run at her with the knife. Seeing her unease made him yearn to do it. He could almost feel how it would be to drive the knife deep into her deliciously yielding flesh. The look of agony on her face would be a joy exceeding anything else in his experience. Killing her was something that had to happen anyway. Why keep delaying the inevitable?

The girl, Kelsey, had been swaying on her feet for several minutes, staring at the door in a drooling, dopey-eyed way that made her look like the recent recipient of a frontal lobotomy. She seemed oblivious to the escalating tension in the room. When the baby cried out again, this time in a particularly loud, distressed way, she began a wobbly approach to the door.

Grant looked at her, frowning. "What do you think you're doing?"

Kelsey continued along her unsteady trajectory toward the door without saying anything or even glancing at him.

Lindsey heaved an exasperated sigh. "For fuck's sake, just kill her and be done with it."

Grant did not want to do that. He wanted Kelsey alive when the time came to act out his fantasies with her. The experiment with necrophilia Lindsey had suggested remained a line he wasn't willing to cross. He was clearly a terrible person perfectly willing to do many things the vast majority of people would consider vile, but the idea of fucking a corpse still grossed him out on a basic, reflexive level.

Lindsey stamped a foot on the floor. "Don't let her open that fucking door! What the hell are you waiting for?"

Despite the increasing gravity of the circumstances, Grant almost laughed. He'd asked himself the same question just moments ago, albeit in a different context. Lindsey was right, though. He couldn't let Kelsey open the door. They still didn't know what they were dealing with here. Someone with sinister intent could be somewhere outside the cabin, and giving whoever it was an easy way in would be a really bad idea.

Kelsey was only a few feet away from the door now, reaching for the doorknob with a shaky hand. Grant moved to intercept her, putting a hand on her shoulder and stopping her in her tracks.

She muttered something indistinct under her breath.

Grant frowned as he began to turn her toward him. "I'm sorry, I didn't get that. What the fuck did you say?"

The girl sneered as she lifted her chin to look Grant straight in the eye. "I said, fuck you, motherfucker."

Her right hand shot toward him before he could react and he screamed when he felt something hard and sharp punch into his groin. He reeled away from her and looked down, shocked to see one of the big nails protruding from his ball sack. Even in the midst of his pain, he realized what must have happened. After extracting the nail from her face, he'd thoughtlessly cast it aside. When he dumped her on the floor earlier, she must have landed near the discarded nail, perhaps palming it while their attention was distracted by the cries of the infant. And now he was paying the price for those moments of distraction, and for not taking her seriously as a threat.

Kelsey again began heading toward the door, but Grant was in no condition to do anything about it. He screamed again when he gripped the head of the nail and began trying to pull it free. Tears streamed down his eyes as he realized how deeply inside him she'd driven it. He'd never known pain like this, not even close. Until now, he'd thought of the pain they'd been inflicting on their captives in an abstract way, but now he grasped the reality of it. It was horrendous and it made him whimper ceaselessly as he pulled harder at the nail.

After gaping in disbelief at his injury for several moments, Lindsey belatedly leapt into action, taking a run toward the door as Kelsey's hand was curling around the doorknob. She looped the belt around the girl's neck and roughly yanked her backward.

She was still dragging her away from the door when Kelsey's mother let loose a muffled scream, causing Grant's head to snap in her direction. The nail was about halfway out now, but what he saw then made him pause in the process of removing it. While they'd been occupied with other things, the woman had managed to pull her foot free of the other nail. She tried to stand in a semi-erect way, but it was impossible. There was too much duct tape strapping her ankles to the legs of the chair. It was a valiant effort, but she was still far from a real threat. She screamed again as the chair toppled sideways, landing on the floor with a heavy thump.

After an agonizing stretch of time that felt like forever but was probably less than a minute, Grant got the nail pulled out in time to watch Lindsey dump the girl on the floor again and scoop up the knife he'd dropped. His gut clenched for a second as he anticipated her attacking him with it. Instead, she rushed over to Piper Weatherby, dropped to a knee next to her, and slammed the big knife into her midsection several times in rapid succession. Her face was red and she was breathing heavily as she almost immediately bounced back to her feet and looked at Grant.

"So much for the mother," she said, sneering. "Now for the daughter."

Kelsey was beginning to get to her hands and knees again as Lindsey approached her.

"*No!*" Grant screamed at her.

Lindsey stopped in her tracks, giving him a confused look. "Why the fuck not?"

Grant whimpered as he held his balls with a trembling hand, watching as blood trickled between his fingers. "I haven't gotten to fuck her yet."

Lindsey laughed. "Grant, baby, I hate to break it to you, but you're not going to be fucking anything again for a long time. Maybe never." She laughed again, harder this time, her breasts jiggling as her body quaked with the hilarity of it. "*Probably* never. Man, that bitch really nailed you."

She laughed harder than ever then, almost doubling over.

Granted wanted nothing more than to go over there and start slamming his fist into her face. Over and fucking over, feeling her nose break and pulp and her lips split apart while he beat her to death. It would be exactly what she deserved. Right then, however, it hurt to even move. Beating anyone to death at the moment was about as likely as the possibility of him sprouting wings from his back and flying off to the goddamn moon.

While Lindsey was still in the grip of hysterics, the girl surged to her feet and ran toward the door. Grant reached out to grab her with his free hand, but she easily eluded him. She grabbed the doorknob, turned it, and hauled the door open, letting in the October chill. Grant shivered as the cold air touched his skin. He'd been outside naked not long ago, but at that point he'd been physically whole, a young man in the prime of his life. But now he had blood leaking from his balls and it hurt so goddamn much.

Kelsey stepped outside and knelt to scoop her baby brother off the porch. She had the crying infant in her arms and was cooing at him when a shadowy figure emerged from between the camper and minivan and came running toward the porch. Grant caught a glimpse of him as he came up the steps, a scraggly-looking mountain man with a bushy beard and long gray hair. He was dressed in threadbare, patchy clothes and had the leathery skin of a person who'd lived most of his life outdoors.

The mountain man had a machete, old and heavily encrusted with rust, but the blade was probably still sharp enough to do some damage. He raised it as he stepped onto the porch, and Kelsey looked up in time to see the oncoming threat. She gasped and backed up into the cabin. The mountain man followed her through the open door.

Lindsey scowled at him. "Who the fuck are you, you Grizzly Adams-looking motherfucker?"

The mountain man did not immediately respond. He took a moment to look around at the gruesome scene inside the cabin. Then he grunted and spoke in the creaky voice of one long-unaccustomed to speaking out loud. "I am the rumble of distant thunder. I am a messenger from the heart of darkness. I am judgment."

No one seemed to know how to react to that as a silent moment passed.

Then the mountain man raised the machete and brought it around with the practiced, savage swing of a skilled executioner.

32

LINDSEY WAS SHOCKED AS SHE watched the rusty blade cleave through Kelsey's neck with surprising ease. She supposed the man's raw strength more than compensated for any lack of sharpness in the blade. The girl remained upright a few moments longer, blood spurting from her neck stump as her head fell to the floor, landing with a loud thump. Her headless body moved backward a few wobbly steps before dropping to its knees and toppling over. The crying infant slid from her limp arms and rolled onto its back on the floor.

Grant's blood-smeared hand came away from his mangled balls. He held up both hands now in a desperate warding-off gesture as the wild-looking stranger came farther into the cabin. "We don't want any trouble. Look, you have to leave. This is a . . . a private property. If you don't leave, we'll call the police."

The mountain man said nothing as he took a pointed look around at all the evidence of depravity.

Grant abruptly seemed to realize how futile his argument was.

His shoulders sagged as he said, "Okay. Fuck you, then."

The mountain man grunted.

Then he charged at Grant and rammed the blade into his abdomen, making Lindsey wince as the bloody tip of the blade emerged from her husband's back. His body slowly went limp as the scraggly stranger held him there on the blade a few moments. When the man yanked the blade free, Grant collapsed to the floor and didn't move.

The mountain man turned and looked at Lindsey.

They stared at each other for a time as she pondered what to do. She still had the knife, which was slightly reassuring. It had some real heft to it and having it was infinitely preferable to facing this enigmatic backwoods madman unarmed. Still, the situation boiled down to short blade versus much longer blade. The reach advantage would probably allow him to cut her down before she could do anything to him. Overall, things were looking dire from her point of view. The tranquilizer gun was still over there on the table, though. She might be able to get to it before he could get to her. There was just one problem—she didn't know if it still had any darts in it.

Alternatively, she could try to make a break for it. The mountain man had displayed surprising quickness in the way he'd dispatched Kelsey and Grant, but she was confident she could elude him and outrun him. Hell, she could outrun damn near anyone who didn't possess Olympic-level track talent. Fleeing this place naked wouldn't be ideal, but she'd do it if she had to.

Before she could do any of these things, the mountain man spoke. "I saw you out there." His voice was gravelly, dense, and not easy to understand. If there'd been any other significant source of noise in the cabin, she wouldn't have known what he was saying. "On the ridge. Saw you kill that boy. Saw you leave the little one. Devil's work, that was. How mean it was. How cold-hearted."

Lindsey's heart was beating so hard she felt faint. Her head was swimmy and she had to concentrate to stay on her feet. She didn't remember seeing anyone else out there on the drive, but this strange man had been watching her from somewhere, which should've been impossible. There was nowhere to hide out there, no trees to lurk behind. The only thing she could think of was if he'd been hanging down a side of the ridge, just below road level. But that was crazy. The sides of the ridge were so steep and rocky and perilous. Who would do something like that?

But the answer to that was obvious, wasn't it?

A crazy person would do that.

Coincidentally, a crazy person was standing in front of her right now, staring at her in a strangely expectant way, as if waiting for her to say something. She didn't get it. Did he expect her to defend what she'd done?

The mountain man spoke again while she was still scrambling for something to say. "Many years ago, after getting out of penitentiary that last time, I did some cold-hearted things, too. I had the voice of the devil in my head, telling me what to do."

Another expectant silence ensued.

Lindsey swallowed with difficulty. "What . . . what kind of cold-hearted things?"

He might have smiled then, but it was difficult to tell with the thick tangle of whiskers around his mouth. "I murdered my whole family. Butchered them. My wife. My son. Ma and Pa. One cold night when the thunder was so loud I thought it would crack my head open."

Lindsey let out a breath and kept working hard to maintain some semblance of composure. "Okay, so I've done bad things. You have, too. So we're, what . . . sort of even, right? We could both just walk away from this, pretend it never happened."

The mountain man shook his head. "The devil doesn't want that. He wants something else of us."

Lindsey made an exasperated sound. "And what, pray tell, would that fucking be?"

This time he definitely smiled, his mouth opening wide to reveal several gaps between the remaining rotten yellow teeth. "The devil says I've been alone too long. That it's time I took a bride."

He took a step toward her.

That decided things for Lindsey. It was time to bolt.

She gave the mountain man as wide a berth as she could manage as she made a break for the open door, but he again surprised her with his preternatural quickness, stopping her cold when he snagged hold of her wrist. She cried out in surprise and pain and tried swiping at him with the knife. He sent the knife flying from her hand with a flick of the machete. It landed on the floor with a clatter, sliding well out of reach beneath the table. She tried twisting out of his grip and flailing against him, but he held her in place with effortless ease.

His mouth opened wider as he pulled her close, causing her to gag at his rancid breath. "I've seen the way you can fly, little lady. I'll take you as my bride, but I can't have you running out on me. And there's only one way of dealing with a woman inclined to run. You gotta make it so she *can't* run."

Another swing of the machete took her left arm off a few inches below the shoulder. She screamed even before the pain hit her and screamed again when it did. It was so much worse than she'd ever imagined something like that would be. The arm the blade had taken was the one he'd been gripping by the wrist. He tossed it aside as she wheeled away from him, spraying blood all over the floor from her arm stump. She tried running for the door again, but did so blindly this time, tripping over the body of the headless girl.

The mountain man grabbed hold of her by an ankle and dragged her to an open area of the floor, turning her onto her stomach so he could pin a knee to the small of her back. He pulled a rough leather cord from an inner pocket of his coat and tied it around her arm stump, cinching it painfully tight to stem the flow of blood. Even through the overwhelming pain, there was a faint sense of relief in knowing she wasn't going to bleed out right away.

Then he raised the machete again and brought it down

Lindsey screamed again as the blade chopped through her right arm and bit into the wooden floor beneath. He still had her pinned to the floor as he produced another of the leather cords from his jacket and tied-off the second arm stump. As he climbed off her, Lindsey had a pretty good idea what was coming next. It terrified her, but she was now beyond powerless to stop it.

Two more efficient swings of the machete removed her feet just above the ankles. Lindsey was crying ceaselessly by then and begging for mercy. Again, he used rough leather cords to tie off the stump wounds.

His knees creaked as he flipped her onto her back and got to his feet. He smiled again as she looked up at him and tearfully pleaded for her life.

"I done told you, pretty lady. I'm not gonna kill you. You're my bride. And this here's our wedding night. Now, don't worry none. We'll cauterize them stumps and give you plenty of healing time before we consummate the marriage." He indicated the squalling infant and the headless body of the girl with separate tilts of his chin. "A man has needs, of course. Tonight I'll spill my seed in Ichabod Jane over there. The baby will give us a head start on the big ol' family we're gonna have together. Smile, girl. This is a *happy* night."

Lindsey started screaming then and didn't stop until her lungs were raw.

The mountain man went into the kitchen to turn on the stove.

33

PLAYING DEAD WAS THE ONLY method of protection available to Jorge when the mountain man invaded the cabin. He tried his best to remain absolutely still and not make a sound, an effort that included making his breathing as shallow as possible. Forcing himself not to cough was the hardest part, as having the woman's panties lodged in his mouth meant his gag reflex was close to being triggered almost constantly. Somehow, however, he managed to keep the urge in check, though he endured countless close calls. The easiest part was controlling the pain. After enduring such extreme levels of agony throughout the evening, it wasn't difficult to relegate the current somewhat lesser level of steady throbbing to the background.

At no point did he truly believe the effort would succeed. He expected the wild-looking stranger to check him out in at least a cursory way at some point, probably killing him after confirming he was still among the living, but that did not happen. The man being so intensely focused on the woman who shot Jorge with the tranquilizer gun at the start of this long nightmare was another big factor in his survival. Also, at a glance, he probably looked dead, with his face covered in dried blood and another person's scalp stitched to his head. The guy probably gave him one look, dismissed him as already gone, and kept his attention on more interesting pursuits.

Playing dead did not prevent him from occasionally glimpsing the atrocities taking place in the cabin. He watched surreptitiously through slitted eyes whenever he could, closing them completely any time he sensed the intruder might turn in his direction. Observing events this way meant he missed some things, but he saw more than enough to confirm the invader was at least as deranged as his abductors, perhaps even more so. Not too long ago he would've found the concept of anyone more evil than the sadistic young couple difficult if not impossible to believe.

Then he watched in sickened disbelief as the stranger methodically amputated Lindsey's limbs and quickly applied makeshift tourniquets to all of them to keep her from bleeding out. He watched again as the mountain man disrobed and copulated with the headless corpse of the younger girl while the stove was heating up in the kitchen. Then came the stench of burning human flesh as Lindsey was dragged screaming into the kitchen to have her stumps cauterized.

Jorge felt no compassion or sympathy for Grant and Lindsey. They were evil people who'd caused him tremendous pain and richly deserved the suffering they received in return. His hatred of them, however, did not make him blind to the inhuman actions of the deranged stranger. They were vile acts only a monster in human guise could perform. The man had said something about the devil talking to him in his head. After all he'd seen and heard, Jorge found that easy to believe.

The young girl's fate was another matter. While she'd done a horrendous thing to him, he did feel some level of sympathy for her. She wasn't much more than a kid, really. A terrified kid who felt compelled to do awful things in exchange for a promise of continued survival. She wasn't entirely without blame, of course, and there was definitely a limit to his sympathy, but she'd been tortured and threatened without mercy. There weren't many people in this world who could go through what she had and come out of it smelling like roses.

At some point, the mountain man dragged Lindsey outside. Jorge could still faintly hear her sounds of suffering, but they were muffled now, as if they were coming from inside a box or coffin. The more likely explanation was that he'd stashed her in one of the vehicles outside. Jorge hoped he would soon hear the sound of an engine starting up and then driving away, but that didn't happen.

Within a few minutes, the mountain man came back into the cabin. At that point, he was still naked, his filthy old clothes discarded in a pile on the floor. He did not put them back on, choosing instead to spend a significant amount of time ransacking the place, downstairs and upstairs. At one point, Jorge heard a sound of water running and guessed the man was taking his first shower in possibly decades.

Jorge tried his best to remain alert while all this was happening, but he soon found himself drifting back toward unconsciousness. He did his best to pull himself back from the brink numerous times, but eventually he succumbed and fell into a state of deep sleep.

When he next awakened, the first faint rays of dawn were visible through the window by the door. He squinted his eyes against the light until they adjusted and instinctively tried to yawn, instead gagging on the panties still in his mouth. Grimacing, he realized how fortunate he was not to have choked to death on them while he was asleep. It was something of a miracle it hadn't happened.

Once he was no longer squinting, he spent some time assessing the situation as best he could given his current limitations. Obviously several hours had passed, something he would have guessed even without the dim light coming through the window. He could tell in his body, in his bones, and in the renewed strength in his muscles. The pain was still ever-present and significant, but there was no denying the difference the hours of sleep had made. He felt ready to fight for his life again, which he had every intention of doing given even half a chance.

The mountain man's grubby old clothes were still in a discarded heap on the floor, but there was no other indication he might still be around. The girl's headless body was no longer in its former position on the floor, nor was her head. The corpse had either been moved elsewhere in the cabin, dragged and dumped outside, or the stranger had taken it with him. The latter possibility assumed he'd already permanently departed the premises, but that was still far from an established fact.

Jorge listened intently for several minutes, straining to detect even the slightest sound of human activity inside the cabin, but there was nothing. The floorboards and stairs here creaked a lot. If anyone was up and moving around, there would be some noise. It didn't take much longer for Jorge to determine he was the only person still alive in the cabin.

Once he'd come to this conclusion, he decided the time had come to put everything he had into freeing himself from the chair. It wouldn't be easy. In fact, it might wind up being the hardest thing he'd ever had to do. Doing it would mean an instant and prolonged intensification of the pain. There would be moments of agony so severe it would feel unbearable. Nevertheless, he had to do it, had to find the inner strength to break the Mendez curse.

The worst part would be pulling his feet free of the nails. The girl's mother had done it, and if she could do it, so could he. A big part of how she'd accomplished it was, of course, down to maternal instinct, a relentless drive to do whatever it took to protect her surviving children. He didn't have anything like that as an extra motivating factor. His desire to keep on living would have to be enough. Plus he still wanted to see his dog again. Rex. He was such a good boy.

Just start doing it, he told himself. *The longer you wait, the worse it'll be.*

After allowing himself one last moment to get ready for the pain, he flexed the toes of his right foot—a movement that by itself triggered a stinging lash of agony—and began trying to lift the foot off the floor. He encountered resistance in the form of the head of the nail seconds after his foot began to slide up the thick length of steel. The pain was even worse than he imagined. He screamed. He wept. He begged for help that wouldn't be coming. He cried out for his momma. He cried out for Rex. And then he tried lifting his foot again.

The head of the nail began to sink beneath the flesh at the top of his foot, but only by about a millimeter or two. At that point, he could raise it no higher no matter how hard he tried, a realization that caused him to scream in frustration and despair. The problem was simple. As their first captive—and only planned captive at that point—the couple had taken a greater level of care in securing him to the chair. They took their time with it and used far more duct tape than they later used with the girl's mother. His legs were too effectively immobilized to raise his foot beyond the current level.

There was nothing he could do.

He was going to die in this fucking chair.

Just as he was beginning to feel resigned to this sad fate, another possibility occurred to him. His heart started beating faster again as he weighed the viability of what he had in mind. It might work. It might not. Probably not, but that didn't matter. It was his final option, of that he had no doubt.

After again steeling himself for an explosion of pain, he rocked himself forward slightly, causing the chair's back legs to raise off the floor by an inch or two. His hope was this would provide the necessary extra leverage to accomplish what he had in mind.

Only one way to find out.

He abruptly threw the chair backward with as much force as he could muster, causing the nail heads to tear through the tops of his feet, further splintering bones while shredding tendons and cartilage.

Unfortunately, he was not able to tear his feet all the way free of the nails on this attempt. He screamed as the chair tipped forward again and the bottoms of his feet again touched the floor. Instead of dispiriting him further, however, this failed attempt only added fuel to his rage and strengthened his determination. Screaming again, he rocked the chair forward slightly in the same manner as before, then immediately threw it backward again.

This time it worked.

His feet ripped free of the nails and the chair fell over backward. He screamed again, this time in triumph as the weak chair leg he'd detected earlier splintered and snapped. Now he had a greatly expanded range of motion with his left leg. The good news didn't stop there. The chair's back had also broken in the fall. He still had work to do, but he could almost taste his freedom and he wasn't about to let anything stop him from reaching out and grabbing it.

He started thrashing against the broken remnants of the chair. His hands being bound behind his back remained a serious problem at first, but not long after he began shedding broken pieces of the chair, he was able to get to his feet and stand in a hunched-over way. It was awkward as hell and he couldn't move about very well, but it still had to count as a major breakthrough. He was vibrating with exhilaration over what he'd managed to do so far, but he also knew he wouldn't be getting very far unless he could get free of the duct tape.

Moving in a vaguely turtle-like manner, he was able to make his way over to the table, the surface of which was crowded with other intended instruments of torture the couple had never gotten around to using on him. A number of them would've been useful if he'd even had the use of his fingers, but he did not. His hands remained thoroughly encased in many layers of duct tape. He had tears in his eyes as he eyed the handsaw with particular longing.

Jorge spent the next several minutes trying to brainstorm possible solutions to his dilemma. He wound up screeching in frustration, utterly unable to conceive of a way he might use any of the numerous edged tools to cut himself loose from the duct tape without the full use of his hands.

Only then did he become fully aware of the unusual level of heat emanating from the kitchen. It was a thing he'd previously been dimly cognizant of because he was preoccupied with other things, but now it soared to the forefront of his consciousness. Frowning, he began waddling his way over to the kitchen nook. He was maybe a dozen feet away when he first glimpsed the orange glow of the stovetop burners. The obvious explanation occurred to him immediately—the mountain man had never turned the stove off after cauterizing Lindsey's stumps.

Soon Jorge was standing in front of the stove, staring at the glowing burners at about eye level. It was the best he could do while still strapped to the remnants of the chair. The heat coming off the burners was intense and the air above the stove looked hazy, which was troubling. His excitement level was high again, because now, at last, a new plan came to him, one he believed might work. It was a plan with a high level of inherent injury risk, but at this point the potential for further injury meant nothing to him. No matter what, he wasn't getting anywhere without enduring a little more pain.

He turned about and put his back to the stove, grimacing and grunting as he struggled to lift his tape-covered hands high enough to move backward and hold them above one of the burners. The best he could do was get the encased hands flat on the surface of the stove. The muscles in his arms and shoulders strained mightily as he tried his hardest to lift his hands just one inch higher. When he accepted that he wouldn't be able to do it, he did the only thing he could—he slid his hands backward until the layers of tape covering his knuckles touched the closest burner.

The tape began to crackle and melt almost immediately. The burning tape gave off an awful, toxic-smelling odor as fumes began to fill the kitchen nook. Jorge flexed his wrists and strained to pull them apart as the tape continued to melt. It took many more seconds of constant contact with the burner, but the tape finally melted enough that he was able to pull his hands apart. The melted tape burned his flesh as he worked furiously to strip it free of his hands.

He staggered forward, away from the stove, with much of the gooey, melted tape dripping from his fingertips, sizzling as the grayish lumps hit the floor. After flinging these bits of tape away, he went to work hurriedly removing the remaining pieces of the chair still attached to him. In another couple of minutes, he was completely free of the chair and his remaining bonds.

Jorge wanted to weep in joy, such was the intensity of the relief he felt. He'd accomplished something truly incredible, defying astronomical odds. There was reason to celebrate, but now was not the time. Though it no longer seemed likely, the mountain man might yet return. Jorge wanted to be far away from the cabin if that happened. Also, he'd suffered a wide range of severe injuries. Getting to a hospital to receive emergency treatment as soon as possible was now his top priority.

Walking on his injured feet caused him excruciating pain, but he wasn't about to let that stop him. Someone—the mountain man, presumably—had closed the front door while Jorge was still asleep. Now he opened it and peered outside. The remaining tinges of darkness continued to seep out of the sky as dawn began to yield to sunrise.

As he'd suspected, the old truck, along with its attached camper, was gone, but a minivan was still out there in the clearing. Jorge backed into the cabin again, limped over to the body of Kelsey's father, and knelt next to it, gritting his teeth and squealing in pain again as the muscles in his injured feet flexed and strained. He was whimpering as he searched the dead man's pockets for his keys, but he experienced a moment of wild joy again when he found what he was looking for.

Before leaving, he spied his scalp on the floor near the dead mother's body. He scooped it up and carried it with him as he went outside. It was almost certainly beyond salvaging at this point, but on the off-chance he might be wrong about that, he figured he should take it with him anyway.

He got behind the wheel of the minivan, put the key in the ignition, and started the engine. Working the gearshift and spinning the steering wheel, he got the vehicle turned around and pointed toward the way out. Before long, he was cautiously driving the minivan along the winding and perilous private drive. He'd been unconscious for the drive up to the cabin, so he hadn't quite been mentally prepared for how harrowing the journey back out to the road would be, but somehow he managed to keep from driving the minivan off a side of the ridge.

An arm-bar gate was standing open at the end of the drive. It looked damaged, as if the mountain man had smashed through it with the truck. Jorge spent a moment wondering in which direction the madman might have gone, but decided it was another thing that didn't matter. He doubted he'd be running into the man again regardless of which way he'd gone.

Taking a right out onto the road, he hit the accelerator, quickly picking up speed. Home was back the other way, but the closest hospital capable of dealing with the unusual level of trauma he'd endured was in this direction. He'd worry about alerting family members to his condition once he was in the hands of professionals.

He'd gone maybe three-quarters of a mile when an abrupt burst of siren noise made him jump in his seat. A glance at the rearview mirror revealed the flashing lights of a highway patrol car. Jorge felt a flicker of trepidation. He badly wanted to get to the hospital as fast as he could. On the other hand, he knew he was only marginally functional at this point. Letting the cops take over now might be for the best. He might wind up getting the help he needed even faster.

After pulling over to the road's shoulder, he hit the button to lower the driver's seat window and cut the engine. He leaned back in his seat with a groan and closed his eyes while he waited for the officer to approach. Despite the crippling pain, he felt a strange level of contentment. He'd exposed the Mendez family curse as the ridiculous myth it had always been. He'd never feel haunted by it again.

His eyes snapped open a few minutes later when a gruff voice asked him, "What the fuck kind of unholy abomination are you?"

Jorge gasped when he turned his head and saw the barrel of a gun pointed at his face. His brow creased in genuine puzzlement. "Why are you pointing that at me? I haven't done anything wrong."

The officer was tall and broad-shouldered. His arms had the corded muscles of a dedicated weightlifter. Mirrored sunglasses hid his eyes and short tufts of blond hair were visible beneath the brim of his hat. A corner of his mouth curved in what looked like a perma-smirk.

The smirk deepened. "I'll be the judge of that, Pancho."

"My name's not—"

"Shut up."

The officer dipped his head lower and leaned closer to peer in at the minivan's interior. "What is that on the passenger seat? Is that . . ." He took a hand away from the gun to remove his sunglasses, revealing piercing blue eyes. "My fucking god, is that a human scalp?"

Jorge was starting to get scared. He was sweating and his heart was galloping. For some reason, he thought about Rex, saw his sweet doggy face in his head. Why was this happening? Couldn't this man see what kind of hell he'd been through? "Officer, I can explain."

The officer slid his sunglasses back into place. "I don't need an explanation. I've seen enough."

He touched something on his tan uniform shirt.

Jorge frowned. "What did you just do?"

"Turned off my body cam."

"But—"

The officer's smirk was back. "This is why I love my job, opportunities like this, where I can dispense justice and spare the public the expense of an unnecessary trial."

Jorge Mendez never heard the gunshot that blew apart his head and ended his life.

Around the same time Jorge was breathing his last, a fire ignited in the kitchen of a nearby cabin. It took some time for anyone to notice smoke from the fire and summon first responders. By the time they arrived, the cabin had burned to the ground. The bodies of the dead inside were soon discovered and, following a brief investigation, connected to the motorist who'd been killed while resisting arrest less than a mile from the scene.

From that point forward, Jorge would forever be known as the perpetrator of the so-called "Mountaintop Massacre."

The loud and prolonged protests of his friends and family never made a difference.

ACKNOWLEDGEMENTS

Thanks to the following for a host of the usual reasons and not-so-usual reasons: Jennifer Smith, Jeff Smith, Keith Ashley, Brian Keene, Tod Clark, Paul Goblirsch, Ryan Harding, Matt Hayward, Anna Hayward, Bob Ford, Wesley Southard, Kristopher Triana, Lashon Miller, Carrie Nicely, Andersen Prunty, Brian Picard Sr, Christian Wood, Jordan Lindsey, Joseph Branson, and Scott Berke. Thanks also to the evolutionary forces and human ingenuity that led to the existence of dogs and the invention of beer, hockey, and horror movies.

ABOUT THE AUTHOR

Bryan Smith is the author of numerous novels and novellas, including *68 Kill*, *Slowly We Rot*, *Depraved*, *The Killing Kind*, *Last Day*, *Dead Stripper Storage*, *Dirty Rotten Hippies and Other Stories*, and *Kill For Satan!*, which won a Splatterpunk Award for best horror novella of 2018. Bestselling horror author Brian Keene described *Slowly We Rot* as, "The best zombie novel I've ever read." A film version of *68 Kill*, directed by Trent Haaga and starring Matthew Gray Gubler from *Criminal Minds*, was released in 2017. Bryan lives in Tennessee with his wife Jennifer and their many pets.

Follow him on Twitter at @Bryan_D_Smith and on Facebook at https://www.facebook.com/bryansmith/

Other Grindhouse Press Titles

#026__*Naked Friends* by Justin Grimbol

#025__*Ghost Chant* by Gina Ranalli

#024__*Hearers of the Constant Hum* by William Pauley III

#023__*Hell's Waiting Room* by C.V. Hunt

#022__*Creep House: Horror Stories* by Andersen Prunty

#021__*Other People's Shit* by C.V. Hunt

#020__*The Party Lords* by Justin Grimbol

#019__*Sociopaths In Love* by Andersen Prunty

#018__*The Last Porno Theater* by Nick Cato

#017__*Zombieville* by C.V. Hunt

#016__*Samurai Vs. Robo-Dick* by Steve Lowe

#015__*The Warm Glow of Happy Homes* by Andersen Prunty

#014__*How To Kill Yourself* by C.V. Hunt

#013__*Bury the Children in the Yard: Horror Stories* by Andersen Prunty

#012__*Return to Devil Town (Vampires in Devil Town Book Three)* by Wayne Hixon

#011__*Pray You Die Alone: Horror Stories* by Andersen Prunty

#010__*King of the Perverts* by Steve Lowe

#009__*Sunruined: Horror Stories* by Andersen Prunty

#008__*Bright Black Moon (Vampires in Devil Town Book Two)* by Wayne Hixon

#007__*Hi I'm a Social Disease: Horror Stories* by Andersen Prunty

#006__*A Life On Fire* by Chris Bowsman

#005__*The Sorrow King* by Andersen Prunty

#004__*The Brothers Crunk* by William Pauley III

#003__*The Horribles* by Nathaniel Lambert

#002__*Vampires in Devil Town* by Wayne Hixon

#001__*House of Fallen Trees* by Gina Ranalli

#000__*Morning is Dead* by Andersen Prunty

Milton Keynes UK
Ingram Content Group UK Ltd.
UKHW011835120124
435937UK00004B/231